YORK NOTES

HEROES

ROBERT CORMIER

NOTES BY MARIAN SLEE
Revised by
GEOFF BROOKES

Longman
is an imprint of

PEARSON

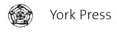

York Press

YORK PRESS
322 Old Brompton Road, London SW5 9JH

PEARSON EDUCATION LIMITED
Edinburgh Gate, Harlow,
Essex CM20 2JE, United Kingdom
Associated companies, branches and representatives throughout the
world

First published 2006

This new and fully revised version 2011

10 9 8 7

ISBN 978–1–4082–7003–5

Illustrations by Bob Moulder; and Neil Gower (p. 6 only)

Photograph of Robert Cormier reproduced courtesy of the Robert
Cormier family

Phototypeset by Chat Noir Design, France

Printed in China (CTPS/07)

CONTENTS

PART FOUR
KEY CONTEXTS AND THEMES

PART FIVE
LANGUAGE AND STRUCTURE

PART SIX
GRADE BOOSTER ★

Study and revision advice

There are two main stages to your reading and work on *Heroes*. First, the study of the novel as you read it. Second, your preparation or revision for the exam or controlled assessment. These top tips will help you with both.

 READING AND STUDYING THE NOVEL – DEVELOP INDEPENDENCE!

- Try to engage and respond **personally** to the characters, ideas and story – not just for your enjoyment, but also because it helps you develop your own **independent ideas** and **thoughts** about *Heroes*. This is something that examiners are very keen to see.
- **Talk** about the text with friends and family; ask questions in class; put forward your own viewpoint – and, if time, read around the text to find out about *Heroes*.
- Take time to **consider** and **reflect** on the **key elements** of the novel; keep your own notes, mind-maps, diagrams, scribbled jottings about the characters and how you respond to them; follow the story as it progresses (what do *you* think might happen?); discuss the main themes and ideas (what do you think it is about? Heroism? Guilt? Loneliness?); pick out language that impresses you or makes an **impact**, and so on.
- Treat your studying **creatively**. When you write essays or give talks about the novel make your responses creative. Think about using really clear ways of explaining yourself, use unusual quotations, well-chosen vocabulary, and try powerful, persuasive ways of beginning or ending what you say or write.

 REVISION – DEVELOP ROUTINES AND PLANS!

- **Good revision** comes from **good planning**. Find out when your exam or controlled assessment is and then plan to look at key aspects of *Heroes* on different days or times during your revision period. You could use these Notes – see 'How can these Notes help me?' – and add dates or times when you are going to cover a particular topic.
- Use **different ways of revising**. Sometimes talking about the text and what you know/don't know with a friend or member of the family can help; at other times, filling a sheet of A4 with all your ideas in different coloured pens about a character, for example Francis, can make ideas come alive; at other times, making short lists of quotations to learn, or numbering events in the plot can assist you.
- **Practise plans and essays**. As you get nearer the 'day', start by looking at essay questions and writing short bulleted plans. Do several plans (you don't have to write the whole essay); then take those plans and add details to them (quotations, linked ideas). Finally, using the advice in **Part Six: Grade Booster**, write some practice essays and then check them out against the advice we have provided.

EXAMINER'S TIP

Prepare for the exam or controlled assessment! Whatever you need to bring, make sure you have it with you – books, if you are allowed, pens, pencils – and that you turn up on time.

Introducing *Heroes*

SETTING AND LOCATION

Heroes is set in Frenchtown, a small town based upon Robert Cormier's home of Leominster in Massachusetts. Much of the story is related in flashbacks to incidents that happened in 1940 and 1941. The main action of the novel takes place after the end of the Second World War in 1945.

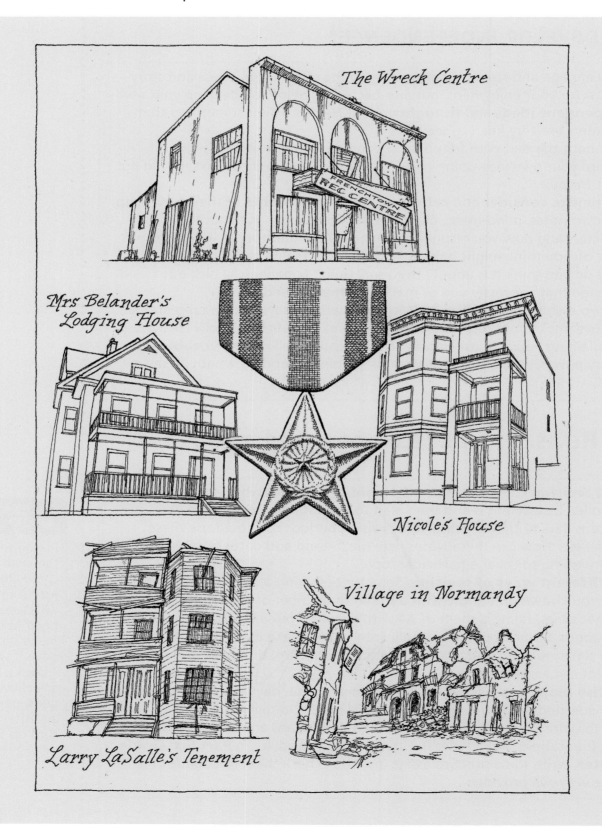

CHARACTERS: WHO'S WHO

JOEY
Francis's friend.

NICOLE
Francis's first love.

FRANCIS
The narrator.

LARRY LASALLE
Youth worker at
the Wreck Centre.

ARTHUR
Francis's friend and
star baseball player.

MR LAURIER
Owner of the shop
where young Francis works.

MRS BELANDER
Francis's landlady.

ROBERT CORMIER: AUTHOR AND CONTEXT

1925	Robert Cormier born 17 January in Leominster, Massachusetts, USA
1939	Start of the Second World War in Europe
1941–2	Studies at Leominster High School, then Fitchburg State College
1941	USA enters the war after Japanese attack on Pearl Harbour
1945	USA drops first atom bombs on Hiroshima and Nagasaki; Second World War ends
1948	Marries Constance Senay
1948–78	Begins to work as a journalist eventually becoming editor of the *Fitchburg–Leominster Sentinel* and *Enterprise*
1974	Publication of first novel for young adults, *The Chocolate War*
1998	*Heroes* published
2000	Dies on 2 November

PART TWO: PLOT AND ACTION

Plot summary: What happens in *Heroes*?

REVISION ACTIVITY

- Go through the summaries below and **highlight** what you think is the key **moment** in each section.

- Then find each moment in the **text** and **reread** it. Write down **two reasons** why you think each moment is so **important**.

CHAPTERS 1–3

- After being badly injured in the war, Francis Cassavant returns to Frenchtown with severe facial injuries.

- He covers his face to avoid recognition and carries a gun with which he intends to commit murder.

- Francis is haunted by his first meeting with a girl called Nicole and his immediate attraction to her.

- He visits the place where she used to live.

- Nicole has left Frenchtown and he doesn't know where she has gone.

- The horror of his wartime experiences returns to him in his dreams.

CHAPTERS 4–5

- Arthur Rivier, an old school friend, introduces Francis as a newcomer to other war veterans at the St Jude Club.

- Francis keeps his true identity a secret.

- Unlike him, the other veterans are optimistic about the future.

- Francis visits the Rec Centre, a youth club which has played a significant part in his life. It was known as the *Wreck Centre*.

- Larry LaSalle is introduced. He is presented as a leader and teacher who becomes an inspirational figure to the young people of Frenchtown.

- An air of mystery surrounds Larry, about whom there are unanswered questions.

- This is the person Francis is determined to kill.

CHAPTERS 6–10

- Later at the St Jude Club the war veterans talk about Larry LaSalle's Silver Star award for bravery in war.

- Arthur Rivier recognises Francis's voice. He cannot understand why, as the holder of a Silver Star, Francis should want to remain unrecognised.

- Francis remembers the time when he won a table tennis tournament at the Wreck Centre and later beat Larry in a match.

- In a flashback to the war we see Francis and Nicole growing closer. At the cinema together they see a newsreel with Larry celebrated as a war hero.

CHAPTERS 11–12

- The flashback to wartime Frenchtown continues.

- After the celebrations for his return, Larry assaults Nicole at the Wreck Centre. Francis overhears the assault but is too frightened to do anything to stop it.

- Nicole is visited by Francis who is tortured by guilt because of his failure to help her. She appears to regard him with contempt for his weakness.

- Later Francis contemplates suicide but instead he lies about his age and enlists in the army.

CHAPTERS 13–14

- It is 1945 again and having discovered that Larry has returned to Frenchtown, Francis visits Larry, in his lodgings intending to kill him in revenge for what he did to Nicole.

- Larry admits his failings and tells Francis he has already made plans to kill himself.

- After Francis leaves, Larry commits suicide.

CHAPTERS 15–17

- Francis visits Nicole to ask her forgiveness and to inform her of Larry's death.

- Although he had hoped to resume their relationship, it is clear this will not happen.

- At the end of the novel Francis contemplates his future and the options open to him.

- Carrying his bag containing the gun which he brought to Frenchtown with him to kill Larry, he boards a train.

Chapter 1: Francis returns to Frenchtown

SUMMARY

❶ Seeking accommodation, Francis Cassavant returns to his Frenchtown home, a suburb of Monument.

❷ He has returned with severe war injuries which are described in detail.

❸ Francis has a strong desire to remain anonymous, covering his face whenever he goes out.

❹ He does not identify himself to Mrs Belander, with whom he rents accommodation.

❺ He pays a visit to St Jude's Church to prepare himself for what he has to do.

❻ He reveals that he is determined to commit murder.

WHY IS THIS CHAPTER IMPORTANT?

A The **opening sentence** ends with the shocking words, 'the war is over and I have no face' (p. 1). This indicates the power of a **first-person narrative** and provides a **dramatic** and **striking** beginning to the novel which immediately engages the reader's **interest**.

B It is clear that the **narrative** will focus on the **relationships** between three characters – Francis, Larry and Nicole.

C We are told Francis **intends** to kill Larry, but we have no idea **why** or what might have occurred to make Francis feel this way.

D We can see that the **action** takes place in the **shadow** of war.

NARRATIVE, LANGUAGE AND DETAIL

The scene is set very clearly and in a shocking way. The use of Francis as a narrator establishes a relationship with the reader. Francis sees himself as an outsider, beyond normal society and normal emotions. He talks about his condition in a detached and unemotional way which contrasts sharply with the details he describes.

Francis does not want to be recognised even though he is in his home town. He is pleased when Mrs Belander hands him a receipt marked *'Tenant'*.

The text is full of references to the destruction of physical appearance. There are references to pain, missing limbs, blindness, disfigurement. The destruction of Francis's face is the destruction of his identity, which is something that he welcomes. These references contribute to the atmosphere of despair which develops as the narrative unfolds.

ST JUDE'S CHURCH

Robert Cormier has chosen to introduce St Jude's Church in the opening chapter to emphasise that there is a moral and religious dimension to the novel. Throughout the novel the central character, Francis Cassavant, returns to the church at times of stress. In Chapter 1 his visit to the church appears to evoke memories of his childhood and perhaps provides him with a sense of security. He prays for his dead parents and his friend Enrico Rucelli.

Francis then thinks back to the words of his teacher: 'pray for your enemies, for those who have done you harm' (p. 6). He has a strong awareness of the rights and wrongs of his behaviour. He refers to his sense of guilt as he prays for the man he intends to kill (p. 7). The planned murder is now his only purpose in life. It is also clear that he believes that he has no future.

EXAMINER'S TIP: WRITING ABOUT THE SHADOW OF WAR

The matter of fact way in which Francis describes his injuries emphasises the nature of war. He hides them in order to protect other people from their shocking reality. He tells the reader he likes to think that the scarf he wears to hide his face makes him look like a First World War hero. Nowhere else in the novel does he talk about himself as a hero.

Before going to bed, Francis studies his face in the mirror and thinks back to conversations he had about his injuries with his friend Enrico and also Dr Abrams, the doctor who treated him. During the flashback account of this conversation there are references to the pain caused by war.

It is obvious that Francis's experiences in the war have been defining moments in his life. He will carry the consequences with him forever.

The reaction of his landlady, Mrs Belander, sums up the attitude of many people towards Francis: 'Poor boy' (p. 3). How do you think Francis would view such a reaction? Would he want to be pitied?

CHECKPOINT 1

Why do you think it is important to Francis to remain anonymous?

KEY QUOTE

Francis (when thinking about Enrico): 'even when he laughed, you could see the pain flashing in his eyes' (p. 8).

GRADE BOOSTER

Writers often introduce characters and reveal the themes of a text in the opening chapter. It can be useful to refer to the opening chapter in an examination answer.

Chapter 2: The arrival of Nicole Renard

SUMMARY

① A flashback to Francis's days at school tells of his first meeting with Nicole Renard.

② They exchange a glance in a maths lesson which means much more to Francis than it does to her.

③ Nicole is portrayed as beautiful and pure; Francis reveals his love and devotion to her right from the start.

④ They meet occasionally when Nicole visits her friend Marie who lives in the same apartment block.

⑤ Francis does not know how to deal with his emotions and is overshadowed by his more confident friend, Joey LeBlanc.

WHY IS THIS CHAPTER IMPORTANT?

A This chapter is devoted to **flashbacks** from scenes of Francis's childhood and focuses on the **attraction** Francis feels for Nicole from their first meeting.

B The central **importance** of Nicole in the novel is established.

C We learn about the **childhood** character of Francis and are aware of how much his **wartime** experiences have **changed** him. His love of reading is displayed: the choice of *The Sun Also Rises* is especially significant.

D This is Frenchtown **before** the arrival of **Larry LaSalle**. We are introduced to other members of Francis and Nicole's **social circle**.

FRANCIS BEFORE THE ARRIVAL OF LARRY LASALLE

The young Francis is revealed in this chapter as a shy boy lacking in confidence. When Nicole looks at him he is unable to speak and merely blushes. Francis is only too well aware of his shortcomings and appears to wish that he could behave differently, 'I'd plunge into an agony of regret' (p. 12) – the word 'agony' suggesting the pain and torture he suffered as a result of his shyness. He doesn't see Nicole as a real person, but as an idealised vision of perfection.

From the moment he first sees Nicole in the maths lesson at school, Francis believes there was the suggestion of the relationship that will develop between them. He refers to the expression in her eyes: 'a hint of mischief as if she were telling me we were going to have good times together' (p. 10). He tells us that he fell in love with her almost immediately. There is a naivety and an innocence in the way in which he views her.

Francis, before the arrival of Larry, is presented as a sensitive boy without the easy confidence of someone like Joey LeBlanc. As he will tell us later, his ambition was to read all the books in the public library. Cormier wants the reader to ask how this Francis became the damaged and vengeful war veteran presented in the first chapter.

THE IDEA OF PURITY

Nicole is presented as an almost virginal figure: 'The pale purity of her face reminded me of the statue of St Thérèse in the niche next to Father Balthazar's confessional in St Jude's Church' (p. 10). The fact that Francis imagines her as a saint emphasises her goodness and suggests that he reveres her and looks up to her; Francis imagines himself as a knight in armour kneeling at her feet. The line 'I silently pledged her my love and loyalty for ever' (p. 10) will become significant later on in the novel when Francis is not able to live up to this pledge.

The reference to himself as a knight reinforces the theme of heroism which runs throughout the novel. It is useful for readers to remember that one of the roles of a knight was to rescue maidens in distress.

THE SOCIAL CIRCLE

Francis is part of a group of young people who enjoy each other's company. They attend school and spend their free time together. We see normal lives and normal relationships, with young people learning about their feelings for each other. This group of friends will fall under the influence of Larry LaSalle. Their lives will be changed forever by the effects of war.

At the end of the chapter we are introduced to Joey LeBlanc. He was a much more confident boy than Francis who was able to shout cheeky remarks to Nicole as she crossed the street. This serves to contrast with Francis's tongue-tied behaviour whenever he met Nicole.

Francis's lack of confidence is reinforced in the final line of the chapter: 'I wondered whether she'd been waving at Joey LeBlanc or me' (p. 15). Think about Francis's place in his social circle and how this changes during the novel.

EXAMINER'S TIP: WRITING ABOUT CONNECTIONS

Making connections between different parts of the book can impress an examiner. For example, consider the association between 'mother' and unhappiness at moments in the novel. Look at the following: page 6 where we are told that Francis's mother died in childbirth; page 23 where the German boy dies calling out for his mother; page 64 where a child cries on seeing Francis and hides his face in his mother's skirt. Why does Robert Cormier do this? What is the effect?

KEY QUOTE

Francis: 'I wanted to shout from the rooftops: "I love her with all my heart"' (p. 13).

CHECKPOINT 2

Make a list of the words and phrases used to describe Nicole on p. 10. What do you learn about her character from these examples?

Chapter 3: The horror of war

SUMMARY

① Memories of Nicole are still fresh in his mind as Francis visits the place where she used to live.

② He recalls a conversation he had with an army comrade about Nicole.

③ Remaining anonymous is still very important to Francis; he lies to his landlady about his name to keep his identity hidden.

④ The horrors Francis endured in the war are revealed through a description of one of his nightmares.

WHY IS THIS CHAPTER IMPORTANT?

A We have further **evidence** of how important **Nicole** is to Francis.

B We find out that Francis joined the **army** even though he was **too young** to do so.

C We learn more about his **direct involvement** in the horrors of war.

THE IMPORTANCE OF NICOLE

The image of Nicole is there in the background in everything that Francis does. He cannot escape from her influence. He is drawn to her old house even though he knows she isn't there. She represents moments in his life which he can never recapture.

During the war in France he met an old friend from home, Norman Rocheleau, and they talked about Nicole. We discover that she was indeed Francis's girlfriend, that something unexplained happened which changed her behaviour and that her family left town suddenly, without warning. This adds to the air of mystery surrounding both her and Francis.

EXAMINER'S TIP: WRITING ABOUT FRANCIS'S EXPERIENCE IN THE WAR

In a nightmare Francis re-lives the occasion when he and his platoon arrived in an abandoned village in France. This illustrates the fear and suffering of young soldiers during the Second World War. His comment, 'not like the war movies at the Plymouth, nobody displaying heroics or bravado' (p. 23) suggests that Cormier wants to emphasise the horror that Francis had to confront. He came face to face with two German soldiers and shot them both, one of them crying 'Mama' as he fell to the ground. The vision haunts Francis. The following day he receives his own terrible injury, which he refers to in an unemotional way.

The chapter concludes with Francis's words to himself, 'maybe this will be the day that Larry LaSalle will appear on the streets of Frenchtown and you will be able to carry out that mission' (p. 25). The word 'mission' is used by the military – you could use this as evidence of how army life has influenced Francis. It is clear that this mission is his consuming motivation. He killed in the war; now he is ready to kill in peacetime.

CHECKPOINT 3

What methods does Cormier use to build up suspense around the character of Nicole?

★ **GRADE BOOSTER**

The ability to examine a writer's use of language in detail is an important skill to develop. For example, look closely at the description of the war episode in Chapter 3 and make a note of the ways in which Cormier uses the five senses to engage readers in the events.

KEY QUOTE

Francis: 'The next day, the grenade blows my face away' (p. 24).

Chapter 4: Meeting with old friends

SUMMARY

① On his way to the Wreck Centre Francis meets Arthur Rivier, another veteran from the war.

② Together with other young men who have been in the war, Francis has a drink in the St Jude Club.

③ He recognises them but they do not know who he is.

WHY IS THIS CHAPTER IMPORTANT?

A We can see how **important** the Wreck Centre is to him and how it is associated with **unhappiness**.

B There is evidence of the **social circle** of which he was once a part. The veterans speak about the **future** in a way that Francis **cannot**.

C The comments about **heroism** add to the impression of Francis's low **self-esteem**.

OLD FRIENDS

Francis thinks back to Arthur's first visit home in his army uniform along with other soldiers and he remembers how he wanted to be like these heroes and how much they impressed him. He also remembers that Arthur was a very good baseball player before he went to fight in the war.

As the other men drink beer and chat, Francis does not join in, although he does state that he wishes he could be part of the 'camaraderie' (p. 28). He recognises them but they have no idea who he is. The veterans are talking about their plans for the future, by taking advantage of the GI Bill.

EXAMINER'S TIP: WRITING ABOUT HEROISM

Different kinds of heroism and different types of heroes are portrayed in the novel. Before he enlisted in the army, Arthur Rivier had been a star first baseman, a sporting hero. It should be noted that Arthur Rivier no longer looks like a hero – 'his eyes are bleary and bloodshot' (p. 26). The war has destroyed his heroic qualities.

Francis was impatient to join the older boys in 'that great crusade for freedom' (p. 27). His idealistic attitude towards fighting appears to have altered considerably. Towards the end of the chapter he states that he is not the hero the others think he is. It is **ironic** that while others respect him as a hero, Francis feels he is not one at all. What does this tell us about his emotional state?

CHECKPOINT 4

Francis refers frequently to his loneliness throughout the novel. Can you find another reference to his loneliness later in this chapter?

? DID YOU KNOW

Under the Servicemen's Resettlement Act of 1944 (commonly known as the GI Bill) soldiers who had fought in the war were entitled to thirty-six months of education or training with financial support for books, fees and living expenses.

CHECKPOINT 5

Why does Cormier give details of Arthur Rivier's baseball achievements on p. 26?

Chapter 5: The Wreck Centre

SUMMARY

1. The violent history of the Wreck Centre is narrated.

2. In a flashback, Larry LaSalle is introduced as a youth worker who reorganises the Wreck Centre and motivates the young people of Frenchtown.

3. Readers are given an insight into Francis's home life with his uncle.

4. Nicole also begins to attend the Wreck Centre and the growing attraction between her and Francis is described.

5. Back in the present, Francis leaves the Wreck Centre to return to his lodgings, he shivers in the rain. The weather seems to reflect his mood of depression.

WHY IS THIS CHAPTER IMPORTANT?

A The **Wreck Centre** was the most **significant** place for Francis at the most significant time of his life. Here the history of the centre is explained.

B We are given more **details** about Francis's **childhood**.

C Larry LaSalle is finally **introduced** into the novel.

D The **death** of Joey LeBlanc at Iwo Jima is another example of the way in which the **war** has **impacted** on Francis's **generation**.

THE LONELINESS OF FRANCIS

In this chapter readers get a glimpse of the lonely childhood and teenage years of Francis Cassavant. His uncle Louis, with whom he lived, scarcely seemed able to cope with Francis – a young boy in need of affection and someone to communicate with. Loneliness led Francis to take refuge in the activities of the Wreck Centre, where gradually he was drawn in after Larry made a speech urging everyone to take part in at least one activity.

Francis lacked confidence in himself and is very honest about his place in the hierarchy of Frenchtown youth. He is lonely and lacks self-confidence, but for a short time he became a hero at the Wreck Centre.

Towards the end of the chapter Nicole is reintroduced. She attends the centre to take part in the dancing group. Francis likes to watch her from afar, admiring her gracefulness. When she speaks to him, his reaction is predictably one of shyness. His comment after their conversation that she 'sent my heart racing and made my knees liquid' (p. 30) indicates that he was now attracted to her in a sexual way. He recalls that seeing Nicole made his visits to the Wreck Centre complete.

LARRY LASALLE

Right from the start Larry is presented as someone the young people look up to and admire. When he introduces himself to the young people of Frenchtown they applaud him. Larry had been both an athlete and a dancer, but it is as a teacher that Francis remembers him, leading classes in crafts and dancing, directing choral groups and organising shows. Yet there is an air of mystery about him, as if he is not what he tries to appear to be.

GRADE BOOSTER

For a quick revision the day before the exam read the first and last chapters of the novel.

KEY QUOTE

Francis: 'I had never been a hero in such places, too short and uncoordinated' (p. 33).

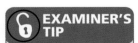

EXAMINER'S TIP

Many students find it useful to make notes in the form of pictures. Make a series of drawings which will help you to remember the **symbols** used in the novel.

There were rumours that he had been a star in New York and Chicago and someone brought in a newspaper clip with a photo of him. However, the young people of Frenchtown were content with the sense of mystery surrounding him as it added to his glamour, even the rumours that he had been in trouble in New York.

EXAMINER'S TIP: WRITING ABOUT THE WRECK CENTRE

This is a significant location in the novel. It is here that Francis develops confidence in himself and his abilities under the guidance of Larry LaSalle. The Wreck Centre forms the background to the developing relationship between Francis and Nicole and the rivalry which emerges between Francis and Larry.

The name of the Wreck Centre establishes the atmosphere which surrounds the building. Like Francis, the Wreck Centre cannot escape from the consequences of its past and the tragic wedding reception where Marie-Blanche Touraine was gunned down by her jilted fiancé. No matter how many attempts are made to rebuild and redecorate the Wreck Centre, it is associated with physical injury and death, and the sense that the truth will always come out: 'The white paint didn't completely cover the dark patches of mildew on the clapboards' (p. 32). The Wreck Centre wrecks lives. The references to guns and disability link the Wreck Centre directly to Francis, and this contrasts with the happy atmosphere created by Larry LaSalle.

At the end of the chapter Francis remembers a comment from Joey LeBlanc that the old sense of doom was still hanging around the Wreck Centre. Think about the effect that Joey's parting words to Francis, 'Doom. Wait and see' (p. 37), and the cold, rainy weather at the end of this chapter have on the reader.

Chapter 6: Francis is recognised

SUMMARY

❶ Francis is now a regular visitor to the St Jude Club where he learns that Larry LaSalle is celebrated as a hero.

❷ He continues in his search for Larry LaSalle.

❸ Arthur Rivier finally recognises Francis, who begs him to keep his identity secret.

❹ Arthur reveals that Francis fell on a grenade and in so doing saved the lives of others.

❺ It is difficult for Arthur Rivier to understand why a hero such as Francis should want to go unrecognised.

WHY IS THIS CHAPTER IMPORTANT?

A The chapter contains **further** comments about the nature of **heroism**.
B The **atmosphere** of the chapter is enhanced by references to the **weather**.
C There is further evidence that Francis has become an **outsider** observing his own life.
D The references to the **future** that Francis cannot share illustrates the sense of **hopelessness** which surrounds him.

ATMOSPHERE

Just as the previous chapter ended with a description of gloomy weather, this one begins in the same way. The reference to the clouds, which are still 'thick and low' (p. 38), could be seen as a **metaphor** for the troubles that cloud Francis's mind.

The weather in Frenchtown never offers any comfort. It is always unpleasant or threatening, either too hot or too cold, as if it is deliberately making life even more difficult for the **characters**.

SELF-ESTEEM

In this chapter it is clear that while others might consider Francis to be a hero, what is most important to him is how he sees himself – a failure with no future. His only motivation is his desire for revenge.

Arthur cannot understand why he will not identify himself. It is clear that something happened to Francis before the war which has destroyed his self-respect. As a result he is full of self-loathing.

The award of the Silver Star for bravery always, and **ironically**, links Francis with Larry. He cannot escape from him. Larry's heroism is celebrated in Frenchtown. The veterans are encouraged to raise their glasses in a toast to him; his achievements are celebrated in a scrapbook of newspaper cuttings. Yet Francis cannot join their celebration of Larry nor can he accept Arthur's praise: 'I look away from the admiration in his eyes' (p. 42). Francis's only focus is his revenge on Larry.

DRAMATIC TENSION

The dramatic tension in the novel centres upon the gradual revelation of what happened to Francis before the war. Robert Cormier draws the reader into the story by revealing the details gradually, allowing the reader to speculate about events and to think about why the characters act in the ways that they do.

We know from the very beginning that Larry LaSalle is Francis's intended victim. The obvious depth of feeling that Francis has for Nicole indicates clearly that she is part of what motivates his need for revenge but at this point we do not know the details and this keeps the reader engaged in the narrative. The obvious sense of love that Francis feels for Nicole is matched by the hatred he feels for Larry.

This chapter adds to the growing sense of intrigue by allowing the characters to speak in praise of Larry LaSalle, whom we met for the first time in Chapter 5 – even the bartender, known as The Strangler, salutes him. We want to know what it is that Francis knows, that the other characters do not.

Because of what has happened to him and also because he is the narrator and our guide to the events of the novel, we feel great sympathy for Francis and begin to feel that Larry must have done something very serious if he has had such an effect upon a character with whom we identify.

Through Arthur, Cormier shows us the respect that the other characters have for Francis and what he did. What interests the reader is that not only does he not share their feelings but also he hates himself. The difference between these attitudes creates genuine dramatic tension.

Everything is carefully designed to make the reader want to find out more!

CHECKPOINT 6

Why does Francis feel it is important for him to stay 'sharp and alert' (p. 39)?

KEY QUOTE

The Strangler: 'To Larry LaSalle, the best of the best' (p. 40).

EXAMINER'S TIP: WRITING ABOUT THE PAST AND THE FUTURE

Francis is unable to move on to the future until he has resolved the issues that haunt him from his past. His refusal to publically acknowledge his identity and his silence mean that he appears to be reviewing and assessing his life as a critical outsider.

Although the talk among the other veterans is about the new life they hope to begin, Francis is not able to take part. It is apparent that, unlike the others, he gives no thought to his future because he doesn't believe that he has one. Yet even though they talk about the future, the other veterans, just like Francis, cannot escape the consequences of the past. The happy atmosphere in the club soon changes and everyone falls quiet as the men appear to be thinking about their wartime experiences. Details are recorded such as Arthur's mouth twitching, Armand staring into space and George Richelieu tugging at his pinned-up sleeve. It shows that Francis is not alone in carrying the effects of war.

Chapter 7: Francis becomes a hero

SUMMARY

CHECKPOINT 7

Find five examples from this chapter of compliments Larry pays to Francis.

1. In another flashback we watch as the young Francis is transformed from a shy and lonely boy to table tennis champion.
2. We can see the influence that Larry has over the young people in the Wreck Centre.
3. Larry makes Nicole and Francis into his special stars.
4. A relationship develops between Francis and Nicole.
5. Larry engineers physical contact between himself and Nicole.
6. Against the odds Francis wins the table tennis match against Larry.

WHY IS THIS CHAPTER IMPORTANT?

A   We can see how Larry tries to **boost** Francis's self-esteem and how Larry's attentions have a **positive** effect on Francis.
B   A **relationship** develops between Francis and Nicole.
C   The **control** and **influence** that Larry has established is carefully presented.
D   We see a sense of **rivalry** between Larry and Francis which is **focused** on Nicole.

YOUNG FRANCIS GROWS IN CONFIDENCE

KEY QUOTE

Francis: 'For the first time in my life, a tide of confidence swept through me' (p. 48).

The chapter begins with a description of young Francis sitting alone on the steps of the Wreck Centre. We see Larry at his very best. Larry has noticed Francis and begun to encourage him, making him feel that he does have special gifts. Under Larry's guidance Francis learns the skill of table tennis. As he becomes a good player, his status in the eyes of the other young people rises and their cheers give him confidence: 'Nobody had ever cheered me before' (p. 45).

As Francis continues to practise table tennis, he is watched by the other young people at the Wreck Centre. When Nicole appears to blow him a kiss, this is a turning point for Francis as he now has some hope that she might like him. Eventually Francis finds the courage to pay Nicole a compliment: 'I love to watch you dance' (p. 48).

LARRY LASALLE'S DESIRE TO CONTROL

KEY QUOTE

Francis: 'I stood spellbound by his words' (p. 45).

The Wreck Centre suits Larry perfectly. It enables him to exercise control over those less experienced than him. He is presented as someone who is multi-talented and admired by all. This gives him power which he exploits for his own purposes. He grooms Nicole carefully, developing her talents as a dancer. As Larry and Nicole dance together, there appears to be a sexual attraction between them.

Larry has the confident belief that everything he does is right. He does not consider the feelings of others. He allows Francis to know that he let him win the table tennis competition. As a result, the moment of Francis's greatest achievement is tarnished because he believes that it might not have been real, that Larry gave the victory to him as if it was his gift to give. He knows for the rest of his life that the brief moment when he was a table tennis hero was not genuine.

CHECKPOINT 8

Joey LeBlanc suggests that Francis has good reason to challenge Larry. What is this reason?

EXAMINER'S TIP: WRITING ABOUT THE RIVALRY BETWEEN LARRY AND FRANCIS

Jealousy towards Larry has already been expressed by Francis as he watches Larry dancing with Nicole: 'Jealousy streaked through me' (p. 46). We are made aware of the closeness between Nicole and Larry in the way their dancing is described. It seems as if Francis and Larry are to become rivals for Nicole's affection.

There is a crucial difference between them. Francis is innocent and inexperienced. Larry is a powerful adult and, as we find out later, ready to exploit the influence his position gives him. Nicole clearly enjoys the attention he gives her.

This unspoken rivalry is sensed by the young people at the Wreck Centre as they shout insistently for Francis and Larry to play against each other. As he starts to play, Francis receives a 'smile of approval' (p. 52) from Nicole. In Chapter 2 Francis had referred to himself as a knight kneeling at Nicole's feet. In the table tennis match it is as if he is a knight fighting for the honour of Nicole. Look at the detailed description of the moves in the game as control passes from one to another and how it helps to emphasise the rivalry.

KEY QUOTE

Francis: 'he caught her, pressing her close, their faces almost touching, their lips only an inch or so from a kiss' (p. 46).

★ GRADE BOOSTER

Consider alternative interpretations for top grades: Larry flirts with Nicole, but does Nicole flirt with him?

Chapter 8: The aftermath of war

SUMMARY

① Francis walks the streets of Frenchtown looking for Larry LaSalle but without success.

② There is a bitter portrayal of a drunken Arthur Rivier, who gives a moving and realistic description of the realities of war.

WHY IS THIS CHAPTER IMPORTANT?

A We can see Francis's **obsession** in his determination to find Larry.

B The theme of **heroism** is given a different **perspective**. Heroism is a mask which obscures brutal reality.

C We have a further example of how Francis observes the **fate** of his generation in a **detached** way.

FRANCIS AS A NARRATOR

KEY QUOTE

Armand: 'Poor Arthur' (p. 56).

Cormier uses Francis's anonymity and secretiveness as a narrative device as well as an authentic part of his **character**. Francis can see his generation and reflect upon what has happened to them in a detached way. His mission means that he doesn't want anyone to know who he is, so he says very little to the other characters. But because he is the narrator of the novel he comments upon them and their fate. In this way he shapes the reader's response. For example, when Armand helps Arthur away, Armand says 'Poor Arthur', but Francis thinks to himself 'poor all of us' (p. 56).

CHECKPOINT 9

When Cormier refers to 'the sorrow in his voice' (p. 55), what impression is he giving to readers about Arthur's memories of the war?

EXAMINER'S TIP: WRITING ABOUT MASKS

Francis wears a real mask, but in this chapter we see how Arthur has an imaginary one. Behind the positive exterior Arthur is in a state of distress. It is revealed when he is drunk. He is depressed by all the talk of plans for the future among his fellow veterans; all he wants is to talk about the war, 'the scared war' (p. 56).

Arthur questions the concept of heroes. None of them were heroes, not even the ones in the Strangler's scrapbook. They were only ordinary people, 'nothing glamorous like the write-ups in the papers or the newsreels' (p. 56).

We can see the way the war affected all those who were involved and how none of them can escape its influence. It was the key moment in their lives, when they saw and did terrible things. Apart from Arthur when he is drunk, no one wants to talk about it.

KEY CONNECTION

Simon Weston's autobiographies, *Walking Tall* and *Moving On*, tell the true story of how a British soldier dealt with terrible war injuries.

Chapter 9: War fever hits Frenchtown

SUMMARY

1. Back in the past again, as war breaks out in 1941, one of the first Frenchtown men to join up is Larry LaSalle.

2. Plucking up courage, Francis finally asks Nicole for a date.

3. Francis and Nicole gradually become closer.

4. News of Larry LaSalle's award for bravery reaches Frenchtown.

WHY IS THIS CHAPTER IMPORTANT?

A The **patriotic** reactions of the people in Frenchtown give a different **impression** of the **effects** of war.

B We see the **developing** relationship between Francis and Nicole.

C We see Francis **happy** and **fulfilled**.

D It is clear how **Larry** casts a **shadow** over them even though he is not there.

E The role of **young men** in the war is emphasised by Mr Laurier.

PATRIOTISM AND EXAMPLE

In Frenchtown people rush to join the armed forces. They are motivated by patriotism. The war is seen as an exciting adventure. Predictably, Larry LaSalle is one of the first men to enlist. He seems to make the war into his own personal crusade.

Just as young people followed his example at the Wreck Centre, so his enlistment encourages others. The men and women of Frenchtown are described wearing uniform and walking the streets with pride in their step. The town is gripped by excitement. Being a soldier is seen to be glamorous.

The war is presented as a great adventure. As yet death and injury are a distant reality. The news reports are no different from the action movies Francis used to watch with Joey. However, when the young people of Frenchtown go to war, they will confront a reality for which their patriotism has not prepared them.

COMING OF AGE

Mr Laurier's comments on young men fighting are very significant. While they might receive some training, they can never be prepared for the emotional impact of warfare. They are still children. But their world had changed. Francis comments: 'We had discovered in one moment on a Sunday afternoon that the world was not a safe place anymore' (p. 62).

It is clear that it is Francis and Nicole's generation who will suffer. They will do terrible things and have terrible things done to them. Their childhood will end and in some cases, like Joey, their lives will end too.

DID YOU KNOW

In 1943 a German aircraft flew from France to a point 12 miles north of New York City and was completely undetected before it returned. It was too expensive to produce but it revealed the technological capabilities the Germans possessed.

KEY QUOTE

Larry: 'We can't let the Japs get away with this' (p. 57).

KEY QUOTE

Francis: 'the people of Monument jammed the Plymouth to see the town's first big war hero on the silver screen' (p. 63).

LARRY'S INFLUENCE

Larry's desire to control the young people at the Wreck Centre is emphasised when he presents himself to them as a hero in uniform before he departs, displaying a pompous sense of duty and a false modesty.

It is important to him that he is seen to be leading the way. His enlistment is such a significant moment that it was for the young people 'the beginning of wartime in Frenchtown' (p. 57).

Later the cinema audience responds in an ecstatic way to his appearance in a news report. Once again the reader will question why Francis no longer joins in with this hero-worship and why Larry is instead an object of hatred for Francis, thus adding to the dramatic tension of the novel.

There is an ominous reference to the song 'Dancing in the Dark', which Francis sings in an off-key way to try to make Nicole laugh. She was to dance to the song at the December production that was cancelled at the outbreak of war. As we will see later, the song is always associated with sadness and suffering.

EXAMINER'S TIP: WRITING ABOUT NICOLE'S EFFECT ON FRANCIS

It is clear that, at this stage, Francis has moved on from being the shy child who sat alone on the steps. Readers are given hints of his development as an adolescent with normal sexual urges as he holds hands with Nicole in the cinema and she allows him to kiss her.

Nicole is able to make Francis feel that he is special as she compliments him on his skill as a writer. Francis seems to grow in confidence and these kind words have a profound effect upon him.

Francis's security and the happiness he feels as he spends time with Nicole contrasts with the portrayal of Francis as a disturbed and unhappy war veteran, which dominates the greater part of the novel. We are aware of how this is a special moment for him, certainly the most important part of his life so far, and the moment that Larry tarnishes and destroys.

KEY QUOTE

'He saved the lives of an entire platoon … Captured an enemy machine gun nest' (p. 63).

CHECKPOINT 10

Make a list of the ways in which Nicole gives Francis confidence, as described in Chapter 9.

Chapter 10: Francis cuts his links with the past

SUMMARY

1. Francis thinks back to the time in England when he first realised the full impact of his facial injuries.

2. He remembers his friend Enrico talking about his intention to commit suicide.

3. He destroys the scraps of paper that suggest he might be able to construct a future for himself.

4. Francis implies that suicide could be an option for him too after his mission to kill Larry LaSalle has been completed.

WHY IS THIS CHAPTER IMPORTANT?

A We are given **more details** about Francis's injuries and how people **react** to them.

B We are shown the **extent** of the **despair** which consumes Francis.

C The **obsessive** nature of his mission to kill Larry is **emphasised**.

A SENSE OF DESPAIR

Francis is determined to cut off all links with his past life; he burns the address and telephone number of Dr Abrams, the doctor who could have helped him with further surgery, and also the list of veterans' hospitals where he could contact his friend Enrico. Francis recalls Enrico's words as he talked about choosing his method of 'disposal'. Francis reveals he 'had already planned my own method after my mission was completed' (p. 66), sharing the cold, hopeless tone of Enrico's words.

EXAMINER'S TIP: WRITING ABOUT FRANCIS'S INJURIES

Francis recalls what his face looked like when he saw it for the first time. His nostrils are described as being like the snout of an animal. He also refers to his peeling cheeks, his toothless gums, and his mouth and jaws clamped together.

He speaks about the horrible details of his injuries. He accepts them and understands that others need protecting from their horror. Francis himself was shocked by what he saw.

Catching sight of his face has altered the way Francis behaves. He now walks along avoiding eye contact with others and wishing that he was invisible.

Francis has to come to terms with the fact that in 'losing his face' he has also lost his identity. As he studies himself in the mirror he says, 'I don't *see me* anymore but a stranger slowly taking shape' (p. 65).

KEY QUOTE

Francis: 'Why didn't anyone warn me' (p. 65).

KEY QUOTE

Francis: 'I start to close doors. Not real doors but doors to the future' (p. 65).

CHECKPOINT 11

What does Francis mean by 'disposal'? What reasons would he have for feeling like this?

CHECKPOINT 12

Why does Cormier use the word 'bitterly' on page 65? What does Francis have to be bitter about?

CHECKPOINT 13

Why do you think Robert Cormier describes the injuries in such detail?

Chapter 11: Turning point

SUMMARY

1. A hero's welcome awaits Larry LaSalle on his first return to Monument.
2. There is the excitement of a civic reception.
3. The evening is a moment of great happiness for Francis.
4. The Wreck Centre is to be opened for one special night at Larry's request.
5. It is an opportunity to return to the spirit of the time before the outbreak of war.
6. Francis is sent away by Larry at the end of the evening so that Larry can have one last dance with Nicole.
7. Larry takes advantage of the opportunity he has created to assault Nicole.
8. When the music stops Francis overhears what is going on, but is rooted to the spot in panic.
9. When Nicole leaves in tears she sees Francis standing in the hallway and looks at him with anger and a sense of betrayal.
10. Larry behaves as though nothing has happened.

WHY IS THIS CHAPTER IMPORTANT?

A Larry is **celebrated** publicly as a hero.
B We can see how Larry **controls** Francis when he **deliberately** mentions the table tennis competition.
C We learn more of the **dynamic** between Nicole and Larry: Nicole is **drawn** to Larry and yet **frightened** by his confident adult behaviour.
D There is an important **contrast** between the **innocence** of Nicole and Francis and the **experience** of Larry.
E The events in the Wreck Centre are the **turning point** in the novel.

LARRY AS A HERO AND A VILLAIN

The early part of this chapter builds an image of Larry as a hero. His wartime bravery seems a natural sequel to his actions earlier in the novel where, single-handedly, he revived the Wreck Centre and gave the young people of Frenchtown a new purpose to their lives. His heroism has now become a public affair as the whole of Frenchtown comes out to greet him. The celebrations for Larry's return unite the people in a sense of pride. He is at the centre of attention, which is important to him. He enjoys the status he has. Larry returns to Monument to the cheering of crowds. This contrasts with his second homecoming later in the novel. However, the war has changed him and he is thinner.

One of the author's purposes in emphasising Larry as a hero is to create a contrast with his behaviour towards Nicole at the end of the chapter (see pp. 75–6). We realise that he is calculating and manipulative. The comments Larry makes at the reception are deliberately chosen to re-inforce his position. He carefully creates an opportunity that he can exploit. As a result we are aware of the essential contradiction that lies at the heart of Larry's **character**.

CHECKPOINT 14

Why would Francis want to celebrate Larry LaSalle's first homecoming?

CHECKPOINT 15

What do the words 'knife-like' and 'lethal' suggest about Larry LaSalle?

KEY QUOTE

Francis: 'His slenderness was knife-like now, lethal' (p. 68).

KEY QUOTE

Francis: 'I couldn't breathe, my body rigid, my lungs burning' (p. 75).

THE INNOCENCE OF NICOLE AND FRANCIS

United in their admiration for Larry, Francis and Nicole watch from a balcony as Larry moves among the guests. They seem especially close as Francis promises to buy Nicole a beautiful ball gown one day and she leans close to him affectionately. As they dance in the streets behind Larry, Francis promises Nicole 'I'll never leave you' (p. 71). This is deliberately **ironic**.

Larry has arranged for the Wreck Centre to open for one more night. As before, he singles out Francis and Nicole for special attention, referring to Francis as his favourite champion and Nicole as favourite dancer. Francis comments that Larry had been their hero long before the war. Larry makes all the young people feel special by looking at each of them in turn. It is significant that Nicole blushes as he looks at her.

EXAMINER'S TIP

Memorise a few key quotations before the examination. The final line of Chapter 11 would be a useful one to learn: 'It's amazing that the heart makes no noise when it cracks' (p. 76).

EXAMINER'S TIP: WRITING ABOUT THE EVENTS IN THE WRECK CENTRE

Francis is too naive to pick up the signals that something may occur between Nicole and Larry, even when Larry tells him that he wants to be alone with Nicole for one last dance. He still obeys Larry as he always did and leaves. There is 'a pang of regret gnawing at him' (p. 73) but only at leaving their company, which is another sign of Francis's innocent trust in Larry. He is jealous of Larry but this becomes a sense of horror when he realises what is going on. Nicole leaves the room in tears with her clothing in disarray. When she sees Francis standing in the hallway she looks at him with anger and a sense of betrayal.

Francis's innocence and happiness are destroyed at a moment of great happiness for him. It is as though both young people know what will happen and yet seem powerless to prevent it. Nicole is certainly attracted to Larry and while she urges Francis to stay with her, she chooses nonetheless to stay rather than to leave. The events in the Wreck Centre and the casual way in which Larry views them make us re-evaluate his character and help us understand the origins of Francis's obsessive need for revenge. What impression do you form of Larry at this moment?

CHECKPOINT 16

What does the word 'gnawing' suggest about Francis's feelings at this point? Why do you think Francis still feels he has no choice but to leave Nicole alone with Larry?

Chapter 12: Despair

SUMMARY

1. A heat wave settles on Frenchtown.
2. Mystery surrounds Larry's sudden departure.
3. Francis feels guilty after the attack and this feeling stays with him forever.
4. He blames himself and believes that he should be punished.
5. There is an uncomfortable meeting with Nicole where she blames Francis for not helping her.
6. After considering suicide, Francis changes his mind and joins the army.

WHY IS THIS CHAPTER IMPORTANT?

A The use of **religious language** adds to the enormity of what Francis believes he has done.

B We can see that Francis believes he is **responsible** for what happened.

C The clear **possibility** of **suicide** is introduced.

RESPONSIBILITY AND BLAME

Nicole's anger and disgust with Francis is revealed in the vocabulary she uses throughout their brief meeting: 'her voice was harsh', 'anger flashing in her eyes' (p. 79), there was 'no pity in her voice. Contempt maybe' (p. 80). It is obvious that Nicole and Francis can no longer communicate. She calls him 'poor Francis' (p. 80) and dismisses him.

Although Nicole could not have anticipated the attack, we can see that she chose to remain in the Wreck Centre with Larry. However much Nicole blames Francis, she cannot blame him entirely. However, she makes her feelings for his actions clear and Francis is so full of self-loathing that he accepts the blame. When Nicole expresses her contempt for him, he is ready to agree with her. He failed to protect her. Although the word 'rape' is never mentioned in the novel, it is obvious that this is the word which haunts him. It is now clear why he does not value himself and why he has returned, determined to kill Larry LaSalle.

EXAMINER'S TIP: WRITING ABOUT RELIGIOUS LANGUAGE

At several points in his conversation with Nicole, Francis uses vocabulary linked to religion, as if to underline the fact that his conscience is greatly troubling him. Francis has already referred to the hell that he has earned. After Nicole has accused him of doing nothing, he feels as though 'all my sins had been revealed' and there was 'no forgiveness for them' (p. 80). These words indicate that Francis is in a state of great despair and that he expects to be condemned even by heaven. At the start of the chapter we are told of the unbearable heat which gripped Frenchtown. Later in the chapter Francis reveals that he welcomes the relentless heat: 'it was part of the hell that I had earned' (p. 78). These words are very powerful and show the intensity of Francis's despair.

CHECKPOINT 17

What could be the reasons for Larry's disappearance?

KEY QUOTE

Nicole: 'Go away, Francis,' she said. 'Just go away' (p. 80).

EXAMINER'S TIP

Aim to spend 3–4 minutes planning your essay. Write your plan in notes and bullets to save time.

Chapter 13: The return

Summary

➊ Back in the present, Francis learns that Larry LaSalle, now suffering from war injuries, has returned to Frenchtown.

➋ As a result of an overheard conversation, Francis discovers where Larry LaSalle is living.

Why is this chapter important?

A We can see that Francis is **approaching** his moment of **destiny**.
B We start to develop a sense that Larry is **not** what he once **was**.
C We can see the **determination** of Francis at the end of the chapter.

The fates conspire

Francis has often dreamed about seeing Larry LaSalle return to Frenchtown. In his dreams he has imagined Larry as a filmstar-like figure striding along the streets. This is **ironic** as we will see as we learn more about Larry's current circumstances.

By chance Francis overhears a conversation between Mrs Belander, his landlady, and a neighbour, Mrs Agneaux. He learns that Larry LaSalle has returned to Frenchtown. The importance of this news is revealed in the language used by Francis to describe his reaction: 'I hear enough to make my heart begin to race and my flesh to grow warm' (pp. 83–4). It would appear that Francis's dream of revenge is about to come true and his reaction has an ominous ring.

Examiner's tip: Writing about how Larry has changed

The description of Larry and his circumstances in this chapter contrasts with earlier descriptions of him. Mrs Agneaux says that Larry walks slowly as if troubled by a war wound. He is living in an out of the way part of town in a run-down house, 'cheap paint, bought discount, fading already' (p. 84).

We can see how Cormier changes the emphasis in this short chapter. Larry is not what he was in the past. We saw the old Larry for the last time when he assaulted Nicole, but now he has changed and we start to realise that Larry, like Francis, has no place in the present.

Compare earlier descriptions of Larry with those in this chapter and think about the impression Robert Cormier is trying to create.

KEY QUOTE

Francis: 'And I know where to find him' (p. 84).

Chapter 14: The final confrontation

SUMMARY

❶ Francis visits Larry LaSalle, who welcomes him in a friendly way.

❷ We learn the reason why Francis joined the army.

❸ After revealing that he is aware of Larry's attack on Nicole, Francis aims his gun at Larry.

❹ Larry stops Francis from shooting by telling him he has his own gun and has often considered shooting himself.

❺ After Francis leaves, the sound of a gunshot is heard from Larry's room.

> **KEY QUOTE**
>
> Larry: 'One gun is enough for what has to be done' (p. 92).

WHY IS THIS CHAPTER IMPORTANT?

A We are given a more **complete** picture of Larry LaSalle.

B We see that Francis has **not escaped** entirely from his **influence**.

C Francis reveals that when he fell on the grenade he was **not motivated** by a wish to **save** his comrades. It was a **suicide** attempt that failed.

D The chapter provides a **dramatic climax** to the novel and is given an **immediacy** by the use of the present tense.

E Examples of vivid **imagery** add to the **emotional power** of this chapter.

DOES FRANCIS FAIL ONCE AGAIN?

As he approaches the house Francis is calm, 'my heartbeat is normal' (p. 85), but he seems to lose his nerve a little once he has heard Larry's voice inviting him in. He defers to Larry, shaking his hand, though he does refuse to embrace him. He still feels that Larry is always one step ahead of him. We can see that Francis is reluctant to speak about himself, as though this might give Larry more power over him. But the more Larry talks, the more Francis's certainty fades.

> **KEY QUOTE**
>
> Francis: 'I still want to die' (p. 89).

Larry reveals the central dilemma the reader must confront in assessing his **character**. Doesn't the good he did outweigh the bad? Even at the end of his life Larry wants to create an impression and control the actions of others.

As before, Francis does exactly as Larry tells him. Larry orders Francis to leave, speaking as though he is again giving Francis a gift, this time the chance to start a new life.

> **CHECKPOINT 18**
>
> Why does Francis feel he is a fake hero?

THE USE OF VIVID LANGUAGE

The dramatic tension of the chapter is heightened by the language and imagery that Cormier employs. He uses **similes** very effectively. He compares Larry's condition with an old faded photograph. The gun Francis carries is 'like a tumour' (p. 85). Larry's voice is like the cry of a child. The **simile** which compares the gunshot with the sound of a ping-pong ball is a deliberate reference to that central event in the Wreck Centre.

There are references throughout the chapter to parts of the body – heart, eyes, temple, legs, face, chest, fingers, thigh, ears. This reminds us that the bodies of the

DID YOU KNOW

Nemesis is the Greek goddess of divine justice and vengeance. In some ways Francis appears as Larry's nemesis here – his arrival forces Larry to atone for his sin and to take his life.

two characters in the chapter have been permanently damaged. This affects the way they see the world and themselves. Winter, for example, seems to have 'invaded [Francis's] bones' (p. 87) destroying any warmth or feeling he might once have had.

Francis and Larry have both been wrecked physically, emotionally and mentally by that one night in the centre and by the war. We are reminded of how appropriate the name 'The Wreck Centre' has become when we consider how youthful hopes and dreams have been destroyed.

EXAMINER'S TIP: EXPLORING THE CONTRADICTIONS IN LARRY'S CHARACTER

It is at this point in the novel that the truth about Larry LaSalle is revealed. It is now obvious why Larry is interested in the young people at the Wreck Centre, especially the girls. Although he may have wanted to help young people and bring out the best in them, it is clear that he had other motives. This may explain the rumours that surrounded Larry – Joey LeBlanc delights in repeating that Larry had '"gotten into trouble" in New York City' (p. 35).

Larry has been portrayed in earlier chapters as a hero who was admired by all around him. Now that the real truth about Larry is known, it is apparent that he did not deserve this admiration. Although he received the Silver Star for bravery in war, it is clear that as a result of his behaviour off the battlefield Larry cannot be regarded as a true hero.

The extent of Larry's war injuries are revealed. He says he is sitting in the chair because his legs are damaged; clearly his dancing days are over. Dancing represented freedom and flirtation. That has now gone forever. The description of Larry shows how much he has changed.

Larry can only live his life in the past. How do you feel about Larry at this point in the novel? Is it different from a few chapters ago?

CHECKPOINT 19

In what ways could Francis be said to have accomplished his mission?

KEY QUOTE

Francis: 'He [Larry] seems fragile now, as if caught in an old photograph that has faded and yellowed with age' (p. 86).

Chapter 15: Welcome news

SUMMARY

❶ Francis visits Sister Mathilde, his old teacher, to discover Nicole's whereabouts.

❷ He receives the information he was hoping for – where to find Nicole.

❸ On leaving he allows Sister Mathilde to touch his face, but hides the secret of the assault, and his despair, from her.

WHY IS THIS CHAPTER IMPORTANT?

A It is made clear that **few** people are **aware** that the assault took place in the Wreck Centre.

B The way the events in the centre **destroyed** the **happiness** of all those involved is **reinforced**.

C We are reminded that others view Francis as a **hero** but this is **not** how he sees himself.

THE DESTRUCTIVE POWER OF THE WRECK CENTRE

Sister Mathilde indicates that Nicole seemed unhappy when she came to say goodbye, and asks Francis if he knew why, and whether they quarrelled. He cannot say. We know that he is desperate to turn back the clock to the time before the assault but he can never repair the damage the Wreck Centre did to their young lives. Neither of them will ever be the same again.

EXAMINER'S TIP: WRITING ABOUT FRANCIS AS AN UNRELIABLE NARRATOR

When Sister Mathilde compliments Francis, 'You have made us all proud' (p. 95), it is clear that like many others she views him as a hero. Francis's heroism does not receive much prominence in the book because this is not how he sees himself. The story has been narrated to us entirely by Francis himself and so we haven't had a clear or balanced impression of how he is viewed by others.

We could describe him as an unreliable narrator. In Francis's eyes he is not a hero but a failure. He failed to protect Nicole; he failed to kill himself. For these reasons he dismisses the opinions of others. Is he right to feel like this? What effect does his style of narration have on you as the reader?

Chapter 16: The final meeting

SUMMARY

❶ Francis finally meets Nicole.

❷ They talk about happier times and about what happened in the Wreck Centre.

❸ Francis realises that the affection between them can never be restored.

❹ Nicole wishes Francis well and he leaves knowing he will never see her again.

WHY IS THIS CHAPTER IMPORTANT?

A This is the **first time** Francis has met Nicole since his **injury**.

B We can see that Nicole has **changed** just as much as Larry and Francis.

C We understand how **happiness** for the characters exists only in the **past**.

D It is clear that Nicole and Francis have a very **different** view of their **friendship**.

E By the end of the chapter Francis realises he must **leave** the events of his adolescence **behind** him.

THE CHANGE IN NICOLE

Cormier tells us that Nicole's hair is now short and her spirit and liveliness seem to have faded. When Francis asks her how she is and she replies that she is fine, he notices 'the softness is gone from her face and her voice is sharp and brittle' (p. 99). The damage caused by the assault lives in her eyes. She does, however, acknowledge that she was wrong to blame Francis for what happened.

Nicole talks about Larry without mentioning his name. She says that for a while he made her feel special, as he made all the young people feel special. But he betrayed their trust.

Their conversation is stilted and at times there is silence between them. This contrasts vividly with the easy communication they enjoyed originally.

LOVE OR AFFECTION?

At the end of the chapter Francis begins to realise that Nicole does not share the intensity of his feelings for her. She does not take him back as he hoped, perhaps because she was never in love as deeply as he was. Just as Larry was not what Francis believed, perhaps Nicole was not what he had hoped either. It is clear that their meeting has a significance for Francis which Nicole does not share.

Francis comments that she looked at him with affection 'but affection is not love … I knew I had lost her, had lost her a long time ago' (p. 103).

Their kiss does not happen as a greeting. In fact, when Francis first sees her he doesn't know what to do. The kiss is a moment of closure. We are aware that there are now barriers between them. The bandage is a physical one but here are unbridgeable emotional barriers too.

KEY QUOTE

Francis: 'I knew all the time we were talking that we were filling up the empty spaces between us with words' (p. 103).

KEY QUOTE

Nicole: 'I shouldn't have said those things to you that day on the piazza. You weren't to blame for what happened' (p. 99).

 DID YOU KNOW

Revision in several short bursts is more effective than one long session.

It is for this reason that Cormier includes ominous references to guns and gunshots in this chapter.

CHECKPOINT 20

Francis says 'I lost her a long time ago'. When did he 'lose' Nicole? Why does this comment arouse the sympathy of the reader?

KEY CONNECTION

Read Robert Cormier's brilliant novel *After the First Death*. Look in particular at the character of Ben and how he struggles to deal with adolescent love.

EXAMINER'S TIP: WRITING ABOUT HAPPINESS

There are very few occasions in the novel when Francis is portrayed as being happy. These occasions are almost exclusively related to the times when he is with Nicole. In Chapter 5 Francis reveals that it is Nicole who makes his visit to the Wreck Centre complete. In Chapter 7 Nicole blows him a kiss when he is playing table tennis, the start of his brief period of happiness with her.

It is important to the plot of the novel that their relationship is initially a happy and innocent one. That innocence is destroyed suddenly and forever by Larry and so is the capacity of Francis and Nicole to achieve happiness.

Nicole's first words to him, 'You've come a long way' (p. 99), are deeply **ironic** because he understands that he can never return to the way things once were. When he hurt Nicole, Larry took away Francis's only hope of happiness. The present is painful; the future is uncertain. The past is where happiness lies.

Chapter 17: An ending? Or a beginning?

SUMMARY

① Francis sits in the railway station watching people coming and going.

② He thinks about his wartime friends and about who the real heroes are.

③ We see Francis leaving Frenchtown. There is nothing to keep him there anymore.

WHY IS THIS CHAPTER IMPORTANT?

A Francis offers further **reflections** on the nature of **heroism**.

B He keeps **referring** to **Nicole**, and at the end of the chapter he mentions his gun.

C The reader is aware that Francis's **future** is **uncertain**. The repetition of the word 'maybe' adds to this sense of uncertainty.

REAL HEROISM

For Francis real heroism lies in the actions of ordinary people. He remembers the boys he knew in the war, boys he refers to as 'scared kids, not born to fight and kill' (p. 105). In his opinion these are the real war heroes even though they did not win Silver Stars. He has contempt for conspicuous heroism. He knows from his own experience that a person's motives are never straightforward.

EXAMINER'S TIP: WRITING ABOUT THE FUTURE

The reader can only speculate about what Francis intends to do. By leaving Frenchtown he is acknowledging that his own story might be finished. Francis returned to Frenchtown in Chapter 1 because he was haunted by events in his past. By the end of the novel he has resolved his relationship with Larry and he also knows that his relationship with Nicole has ended. There is no reason for him to stay there.

His mask has the benefit of separating him from much of the human interaction which surrounds him. He looks at other people and wonders what their own story might be. Perhaps everyone brought home from the war their own story, just like him.

The young man leaning against the wall is lost in his own thoughts, just as Francis is. Does he have a future? Does Francis? He doesn't know what the man is thinking or what he will do. We are also left knowing nothing of Francis's intentions. What do you think he will do?

GRADE BOOSTER

The title of the novel asks us to consider the nature of heroism. Given what we now know about him, was Francis's attempt to kill himself the action of a hero? What was his motivation?

KEY CONNECTION

You might like to read *A Farewell to Arms* by Ernest Hemingway (based on the author's experiences in the First World War). When discussing novels with Nicole, Francis says this is his favourite book.

GRADE BOOSTER

Francis talks about the things he could or 'should' do next, i.e. become a writer, find Dr Abrams and Enrico, get some treatment. He ends by saying 'I should do all these things', and his thoughts then turn to Nicole. How do you interpret this? Are these real intentions, or merely things he knows he *'should'* do?

Progress and revision check

REVISION ACTIVITY

① Who did Francis live with after his parents died? (Write your answers below)

....

② Who was teaching the maths lesson when Francis first met Nicole?

....

③ Where is the reception held to honour Larry's return from the war?

....

④ Where does Francis go to join the army?

....

⑤ Where does Francis find Nicole when he visits her after Larry's death?

....

REVISION ACTIVITY

On a piece of paper write down answers to these questions:

● Why does Larry try to boost Francis's self-esteem?

Start: *Larry finds Francis sitting alone on the steps of the Wreck Centre. He realises Francis is unhappy because …*

● Why is Francis haunted by his memories of events in the French village during the war?

Start: *The horror of what he did in the war is always in Francis's mind …*

GRADE BOOSTER

Answer this longer practice question about the plot/action of the novel:

Q: Why does Francis decide not to throw himself from St Jude's steeple? Think about . . .

● The way events or actions from the past impact on the present.

● The way events slowly build up to a climax.

For a C grade: describe the extent of Francis's despair. Show how he believes he has betrayed Nicole. Indicate that he understands the shame he would bring on his family. Show how his awareness of young men dying in war influences his actions. Use textual detail to support your view.

For an A grade: make sure that you do all of the above. Make sure you chose relevant quotations to support what you say. You must refer to specific examples to show how the author's choice of vocabulary establishes the atmosphere in this section – words such as 'pitiful', 'disgrace', 'horrified'. Write about Francis's lack of self-respect. You should also go on to show that you are aware of how the book explores different perceptions of heroism.

PART THREE: CHARACTERS

Francis Cassavant

WHO IS FRANCIS CASSAVANT?

Francis is the narrator of the novel. He has returned to Frenchtown with horrific war injuries and his mission is to seek revenge on the man who ruined his life.

WHAT DOES FRANCIS DO IN THE NOVEL?

- He returns to Frenchtown but does not reveal his identity because he is ashamed of his past (Chapter 1).
- His return to Frenchtown allows him to explore his own past and the issues which have shaped him.
- He is lonely and damaged, both physically and emotionally (Chapter 3).
- Through his experiences and attitudes we explore the concept of heroism (Chapters 3, 6, 8, 11, 14).
- The character of Francis allows Cormier to explore the emotional vulnerability of young adults (Chapters 7, 9, 11, 12).
- His life is changed forever by two people who arrive in Frenchtown from elsewhere – Nicole and Larry (Chapters 2–5).
- His love for Nicole is the means by which Larry's true nature is exposed (Chapters 11–14).
- When Francis leaves Frenchtown, we are aware of his tragic status (Chapter 17).

HOW IS FRANCIS DESCRIBED AND WHAT DOES IT MEAN?

Quotation	Means?
'I keep a bandage on the space where my nose used to be.'	Francis talks about his injuries in a dispassionate way. They represent a central part of the book. We are aware of the horror of his injuries and the way they affect others. He accepts them as his punishment for betraying Nicole.
'It would always be Nicole Renard.'	Nicole changes his life completely. She is his first, and perhaps only, love and represents his greatest friendship. He returns to Frenchtown to deal with his guilt for not protecting her.
'I'll buy you one like that some day.'	On the night when Larry returns home as a hero, Francis talks about his future in a positive way for the only time in the novel. His dreams and his future are snatched away.

EXAMINER'S TIP

Short quotations are the most effective. Keep quotations to one line at most.

EXAMINER'S TIP

Don't forget to refer to the writer's use of language throughout your answer.

Quotation	Means?
'I start to close doors. Not real doors but doors to the future.'	The sense of despair that runs through Francis inspires the reader's sympathy and understanding. He did not carry out his first suicide attempt and failed in his second. He suggests that he is heading for a third. He does not believe he has a future since the brief moment of happiness he experienced will never be restored.
'I am tired of this talk, impatient to do what I came here to do.'	When he finally confronts Larry, his single-minded mission appears to have reached its conclusion. This moment has been his only motivation. He seems confident and decisive, although he will once again defer to Larry.
'I wonder what he's thinking of or remembering.'	As a child he lost himself in books. In the last chapter he watches a stranger and imagines his story. He knows that his own story has ended.

EXAMINER'S TIP: WRITING ABOUT FRANCIS

Francis as narrator comments upon the central moment in his life and in doing so is the means by which Robert Cormier explores issues such as heroism, deception and guilt. Ensure that you acknowledge the way in which Francis observes Frenchtown and his own life. You need to show that you understand the effect that Nicole had on him. Francis was a lonely and neglected child and we are told that he never had a best friend.

Nicole opens up a range of emotions that Francis has never experienced before. He once enjoyed the encouragement of Larry and admired him. His attentions made Francis feel valued. In return, Larry destroys Francis's trust, his relationship and his life. Francis believes that he should be punished for failing to protect Nicole. He needs to find Larry and carry out his mission as an act of atonement.

Ultimately, consider how Francis is an outsider, observing his own life and reflecting upon it. Notice how the need for revenge and punishment become his reasons to live.

Nicole Renard

WHO IS NICOLE RENARD?

Nicole Renard is an innocent young girl who is not only Francis's first and only love but also the victim of Larry LaSalle.

WHAT DOES NICOLE DO IN THE NOVEL?

- Cormier presents her as a **symbol** of innocence and purity who is eventually soiled by the actions of Larry (Chapter 2).
- Nicole seems to enjoy the close attentions of Larry without understanding their implications (Chapter 7).
- She awakens love and devotion in Francis who gains confidence through their relationship (Chapter 9).
- She blames Francis for not protecting her from Larry's assault, which becomes the key moment in his life (Chapter 12).
- She speaks honestly to Francis at the end of the book, indicating that their relationship is at an end and that it is time for him to move on (Chapter 16).

HOW IS NICOLE DESCRIBED AND WHAT DOES IT MEAN?

Quotation	Means?
'That would be nice.'	When she agrees to go to the cinema with Francis she transforms him. She offers him the attention and affection that he has lacked in his life so far. She enjoys his company and teases him playfully because he is so shy.
'Stay close to me.'	These words on the night of the civic reception indicate that she is apprehensive about Larry.
'Why didn't you do something?'	In the aftermath of the assault Nicole becomes angry and resentful. She feels betrayed by Francis and has contempt for his weakness.
'Why did you come here today?'	These words perhaps indicate that their relationship meant much more to Francis than it ever did to her.

⭐ **GRADE BOOSTER**

In your notes on Nicole, aim to make comments on the language used in the episodes centred around her. You will notice that the vocabulary is softer and gentler than other parts of the novel.

🔒 **EXAMINER'S TIP**

Think about the way Francis sees Nicole as a fantasy figure. Then consider how Larry sees her in a very different way.

EXAMINER'S TIP: WRITING ABOUT NICOLE

You must show that you understand how Nicole is flattered by the attentions of Larry, who has special status among her friends. She enjoys her friendship with Francis and speaks positively to him, about possibilities and achievement. Her relationship with him is innocent and lacks the sexual undercurrent which is there in the way Larry treats her. The result of Larry's attentions is that her life will never be the same again.

Larry LaSalle

WHO IS LARRY LASALLE?

Larry is a mysterious youth worker who has the ability to find and develop the talents of young people; however, beneath the surface there lies a dark and unpleasant secret.

WHAT DOES LARRY DO IN THE NOVEL?

- He arrives in Frenchtown and creates an instant impression (Chapter 5).
- With carefully targeted encouragement he helps young people find unexpected talents (Chapter 5).
- He is predatory and calculating in his approach to Nicole (Chapter 7).
- He always knows what to say for maximum effect (Chapter 11).
- Larry is celebrated as a hero but he has a fatal flaw (Chapter 11).
- Like Francis, Larry too hides his real identity (Chapter 14).
- Even when facing Francis's gun, Larry shows that he still has influence over him (Chapter 14).
- Larry stops Francis from killing him but commits suicide instead (Chapter 14).

HOW IS LARRY DESCRIBED AND WHAT DOES IT MEAN?

Quotation	Means?
'A tall slim man stepped into view, a lock of blond hair tumbling over his forehead, a smile that revealed dazzling movie-star teeth.'	Larry is established as an attractive and glamorous figure. It is as if he has stepped down from the cinema screen as he will appear to do again later. This makes him a natural centre of attention.
'"Good morning," he said. "My name's Larry LaSalle."'	Right from the start Larry is out to create an impression. He enjoys being the centre of attention and the status his role gives him.
'He was our champion and we were happy to be in his presence.'	He wins the respect and the devotion of all the young people because he is good at the things they admire. As their hero they believe that he can do no wrong.
'He applauded her, his eyes looking deeply into hers, as she lay at his feet.'	Larry's behaviour towards Nicole is an important indication of the way he regards young women. He sees himself as dominant and believes that they should be submissive.

KEY CONNECTION

Read 'The Hero', a poem by Siegfried Sassoon where the mother of a soldier from the First World War and the colonel bringing her the news of his death have very different views of the young man's heroic behaviour.

Quotation	Means?
'"What's the matter?" Larry LaSalle asked.'	Larry has positive qualities. He is generous and sensitive in his dealings with Francis, offering time to a shy and isolated boy and allowing him to become a champion, boosting his self-esteem.
'We have to keep the world safe for these young people – they are our future.'	This is an indication of the way Larry always tries to say the right thing. Ironically, Nicole must confront a hero who in fact represents danger and will destroy her future.
'Sweet young things.'	The words that he uses here reveal his character. The girls he has abused are not people, but 'things'.
'Does that one sin of mine wipe away all the good things?'	This comment might indicate that Larry does not accept the full extent of what he has done. He doesn't regard it as serious since he thinks that it can be excused.

EXAMINER'S TIP

Always support your points about characters with quotations or detailed references to the text.

GRADE BOOSTER

Re-read Chapter 14 and the confrontation between Larry and Francis. What opinion do you have of Larry's final words in this chapter? Think about whether Larry has changed as a character by this point, or whether he is still trying to manipulate Francis.

EXAMINER'S TIP: WRITING ABOUT LARRY

Remember that there is an essential dilemma at the heart of Larry's character. Can we ever take at face value anything that he says? He appears to lack sincerity and honesty. He undoubtedly did many good things in his work as we see in Chapter 5. However, they can never excuse his behaviour as a serial abuser of young women. Through his actions he betrays their trust.

You should indicate that you can see the manipulative elements in his character in his 'grooming' of Nicole. Indicate that he expresses his desire for her in the stylised conventions of dance and then introduces an overtly sexual element.

You must show, as a sophisticated reader, that you are aware that it is difficult to accept anything that Larry says as the truth. Almost everything he says or does is designed to create an effect. Even at the end of his life, when we can see that Larry has changed and cannot face a future as the person he has now become, his desire to control those around him is still displayed.

Notice how Robert Cormier encourages us to look beyond a person's physical appearance. The appearance of some of the characters has been altered forever by the war. We are encouraged to see the feelings of the person beneath.

Always remember that Larry sees himself as a creative figure. In fact he is destructive.

Arthur Rivier and Mrs Belander

ARTHUR RIVIER

Arthur, another ex-serviceman and local boy, was once a star baseball player for the Frenchtown Tigers and Francis remembers regarding him with admiration for his sporting prowess. When he first appeared in his uniform, Francis wanted to emulate him. Arthur recognises Francis but agrees to keep the secret.

- Arthur's **character** is used in the novel as a representative of all the soldiers who have suffered. Arthur deals with the trauma of war by meeting up with other veterans; Francis prefers to be alone.

- He appears to be positive about the future but like Francis he hides the truth behind a mask.

- There is a moving portrait of a drunk Arthur who reveals his true sentiments about the war.

- Arthur draws attention to the cruelty of war which turns young boys into killers.

MRS BELANDER

Mrs Belander is Francis's landlady in Frenchtown.

- She represents the attitude of the townspeople towards war veterans.

- She is kind and caring.

- Her home is a refuge for Francis, the only place he appears at ease.

- She is also part of Francis's past. He used to do her errands and she baked him a birthday cake when he was thirteen.

- The character of Mrs Belander is used as a structural device as she is the person who unwittingly lets Francis know that Larry LaSalle has returned to Frenchtown.

EXAMINER'S TIP: WRITING ABOUT ARTHUR AND MRS BELANDER

Although they have contrasting characters, Arthur and Mrs Belander represent the essential good nature of the people of Frenchtown. They both respond to Francis with understanding and offer their support to him with sympathy and respect.

Joey LeBlanc and Enrico Rucelli

JOEY LeBLANC

Joey is a friend of Francis and they sometimes went to the cinema together. He would get in trouble in school by talking out of turn. The things that Joey says are an important commentary on the action.

- Joey is a confident boy who is the complete opposite to Francis.

- He lives in Francis's memory as a lively pre-war boy. Because he died in the war we cannot see the effect that it had on his character.

- His comments about the Wreck Centre and Larry creates a sense of apprehension.

- He suggests that Larry might not be what he seems.

- His death at Iwo Jima shows us the indiscriminate nature of war, i.e. that war takes lives regardless of character.

KEY QUOTE

Joey: 'Better watch out, Mister LaSalle. Francis has got your number' (p. 42).

ENRICO RUCELLI

Enrico was a close wartime comrade of Francis. He shows great courage and is used by Cormier to illustrate some of the horrors of war. He suffered severe injuries, losing both his legs and his left arm. Although they are very different personalities, Francis and Enrico are united by their terrible injuries and their suffering. He displays a certainty about his future plans which Francis does not.

- Although he does not appear in the main action of the novel, his comments, as reported by Francis, are very significant.

- He is the first to inform the reader that Francis was awarded the Silver Star, of which Francis is ashamed.

- Despite the fact that he has severe injuries, he still teases Francis.

- Although he is outwardly cheerful, his sense of despair adds to the atmosphere of the novel.

- He regards himself not as a person but as something which should be disposed of.

KEY QUOTE

Francis: 'Sometimes I think he talked so much to cover up the pain' (p. 6).

KEY CONNECTION

Read about heroism in war in *The Red Badge of Courage* by Stephen Crane.

EXAMINER'S TIP: WRITING ABOUT JOEY AND ENRICO

The purpose of these characters is to show the awful effects of war on ordinary young men. They entered the war out of a sense of duty but it destroyed them. They are victims, their potential destroyed forever. For Francis, the dead and the maimed always exist within his mind.

Other characters

DR ABRAMS

Dr Abrams was the doctor who treated Francis for his facial injuries and he appears to have had some influence on the way Francis thinks about his disfigurement.

- Dr Abrams does not appear in the main action of the book, but his conversations form part of Francis's memories.
- Dr Abrams's comments to Francis create a grim humour in the opening chapter.
- His positive attitudes about the future contrast with those shown by Francis.
- His words add to the direct and shocking way in which Francis describes his injuries in the opening to the novel.
- Dr Abrams's address and telephone number represent hope and the future. When Francis burns them in Chapter 10 it reflects Francis's sense of despair.
- It is significant that at the end of the novel Francis suggests the possibility of finding Dr Abram's address again.

MARIE LACROIX

- Marie lives in the same apartments as Francis and provides a link between Francis and Nicole.
- Marie acts as a confidante for Francis as he reveals to her that he likes Nicole (see Chapter 2).
- Towards the end of the novel readers learn that Marie has continued to provide a link between the two as she has informed Nicole about Francis's Silver Star for bravery.

SISTER MATHILDE AND SISTER GERTRUDE

- Sister Mathilde is a figure from Francis's past who had an influence on Francis when he was at school.
- Francis visits her in Chapter 15 to ask for information about Nicole.
- It is significant that she reminds Francis that everyone has secrets.
- Sister Gertrude was also one of Francis's teachers.
- As he prays in St Jude's Church in Chapter 1, it is Sister Gertrude's words which come into his head.

UNCLE LOUIS

- Uncle Louis cared for Francis after the death of his parents.
- It is possible that Francis inherited his quiet personality from Uncle Louis, who is described as 'a silent giant of a man' (p. 33).
- Although he provided a home for Francis, cooked his meals and gave him a weekly allowance, he seldom spoke to him apart from asking about his day at school.

MR LAURIER

- Mr Laurier, the owner of the drugstore, is another figure from Francis's past.
- Francis enjoyed working in his store, particularly stocking the candy cases.
- It is a result of this job that Francis becomes closer to Nicole as she buys sweets and talks to him about books.
- Mr Laurier's drugstore is a meeting point and an informal news centre for the people of Frenchtown.
- He comments significantly on the way young men are trained to kill.
- People can keep up to date with the progress of the war as they read the newspapers or listen to his radio.

LOUIS ARABELLE

- Louis is Francis's opponent in the final table tennis match.
- Louis lost the match, ensuring that Francis won the championship.

Minor characters

NORMAN ROCHELEAU, EDDIE RICHARDS, ERWIN EISENBERG, BLINKY CHAMBERS, JACK SMITH, SONNY ORLANDI, SPOOKS REILLY, BILLY O'BRIEN, HENRY JOHNSON

- All of these were wartime comrades of Francis and, with the exception of Norman Rocheleau, were all members of his platoon.
- They are mentioned in Francis's nightmare in Chapter 3 (pp. 22–3) and all either died or received injuries in the war.
- When Francis considers what it means to be a hero in Chapter 17, these are the men he thinks about.

ARMAND TELLIERE, JOE LAFONTAINE, GEORGE RICHELIEU, THE STRANGLER

- These men are regulars at the St Jude Club where the war veterans meet.
- The Strangler is the bartender who keeps a scrapbook of Frenchtown heroes in which both Francis and Larry LaSalle figure.

KEY QUOTE

Mr Laurier: 'A kid graduates from high school, gets six weeks of basic training with guns and grenades ... and five months later ... he's fighting the Japs or the Germans' (p. 62).

GRADE BOOSTER

Try memorising useful words and phrases for writing about Cormier's purpose, e.g. 'The writer intends to ...' or 'The writer's aim is to ...'.

KEY CONNECTION

Read the poem 'Strange Meeting' by Wilfred Owen where an English soldier dreams of meeting a German soldier he has killed in battle.

Progress and revision check

REVISION ACTIVITY

1. Where did Larry work before he arrived in Frenchtown? (Write your answers below)

   ....

2. What happened to George Richelieu in the war?

   ....

3. Who says, 'Is that his real name?'

   ....

4. Whose words does Francis hear when he prays in St Jude's Church?

   ....

5. What career does Nicole suggest that Francis should follow?

   ....

REVISION ACTIVITY

On a piece of paper write down answers to these questions:

● Why does Francis believe that he is a failure?

   Start: *Francis is a lonely and isolated child. His view of himself is changed dramatically by his relationship with Nicole and by his involvement with the Wreck Centre. However, when she is attacked ...*

● In what ways is Enrico Rucelli important in the novel?

   Start: *Enrico is important because he helps to create the mood and atmosphere which surrounds Francis. His horrific injuries show ...*

GRADE BOOSTER

Answer this longer practice question about a character in the novel:

Q: Write about the role that Joey LeBlanc plays in *Heroes*.

For a C grade: write about the character of Joey. Show that he is an opposite of Francis. Write about their friendship and Joey's cheeky confidence. Show the contrast in the attitudes they have to Nicole. Indicate that Joey says things which allow Cormier to comment on the action and set doubts in the reader's mind. Write about the Wreck Centre and Joey's attitude to Larry.

For an A grade: make sure you do all of the above, as well as referring to his death in the war and what it represents. Show how his comments create a sense of foreboding and apprehension. Use well-chosen quotations. Show how Cormier deliberately uses him at key moments in the novel to puncture illusions and suggest that things might not be what they seem.

Key contexts

THE AUTHOR

Robert Edmund Cormier was born on 17 January 1925. His family lived in French Hill, a suburb of Leominster, Massachusetts, USA, so-called because many families originally from French-speaking Canada lived there.

Although he travelled widely, Robert Cormier was content to live and work in the area where he grew up and which formed the background to several of his novels. He never lived more than three miles from the house where he was born. His novels are full of characters who are from a French Canadian immigrant background, just like the people among whom Robert Cormier grew up. His reputation as a writer extended beyond the United States and his work received international acclaim. *Heroes* received the award of *Highly Commended* in the Carnegie Medal awards in Great Britain.

THE SECOND WORLD WAR

The Second World War started in Europe in September 1939 when Germany invaded Poland. By the time it finished in 1945 the war had involved much of the world in the conflict. It was the largest and deadliest war in human history with the deaths of approximately sixty-two million people.

America entered the war in December 1941 after the Japanese attacked the American fleet in Pearl Harbour off the coast of Hawaii on 7 December. There were 2,408 Americans killed in the attack. The following day America declared war on Japan and on 11 December Germany declared war on the United States. American troops suffered many losses in Europe and were involved in the successful invasion of German-held Normandy in France in June 1944 (D-day). The Second World War in Europe ended on 7 May 1945 after the Germans signed an unconditional surrender.

The novel shows us how the war reached out into small towns in America such as Frenchtown, through the number of US soldiers fighting in the war.

LIFE DURING THE WAR IN AMERICA

Once war was declared in America in 1941 the lives of ordinary people changed dramatically. Both men and women were encouraged to join the army. If a young person was under the age of eighteen, they could still join up if their parents signed a permission form. This is why Francis alters his birth certificate.

Because so many American men had joined up there was a shortage of workers. This gap was filled by women doing jobs which they had never done before. Encouraged by their desire to help their country, women worked in factories, as truck drivers, refuse collectors and postal workers.

Fear of air raids, particularly along the Eastern Seaboard, led to blackouts where families had to cover their windows and put out their lights at certain times of the

> **KEY CONNECTION**
>
> There are film versions of three of Cormier's novels: *The Chocolate War* (1988), *I Am the Cheese* (1983) and *The Bumblebee Flies Anyway* (2000).

> **KEY CONNECTION**
>
> Look at scenes from *Saving Private Ryan* where American soldiers are portrayed fighting in France. What similarities do you find with the descriptions of war in Chapter 3?

**DID YOU KNOW**

The battle on the island of Iwo Jima on 19 February 1945 enabled the Americans to gain a foothold on mainland Japan. On 15 August 1945 Japan surrendered to the Americans after the dropping of atomic bombs on the Japanese cities of Hiroshima and Nagasaki.

KEY QUOTE

Francis: 'But tomorrow was 7 December 1941' (p. 45).

night. In order to receive news of the war, families would listen to the radio every night or go to the cinema every week to watch the Movietone News.

Robert Cormier did not fight in the Second World War because of his poor eyesight. He studied during the day and worked in a local factory in the evening. However, many people in his home town were involved in the war and, just as Francis and Nicole did, he followed the progress of the war on the Movietone News at the cinema.

SETTING AND PLACE

The events of *Heroes* are firmly rooted in Frenchtown and the effects the war had on the young people who lived there. We only have glimpses of the world outside the community in the cinema or in Francis's nightmares. These nightmares show that Francis cannot escape the horror of war even in Frenchtown. On these occasions he is transported back to the village in France where he killed German boys like himself and was injured by a grenade.

We are aware of how the war reached into the Frenchtown community and affected so many lives, and destroyed so many hopes, even though it was a long way away from the battlefields of the Second World War. After Francis wins the table tennis championship at the Wreck Centre and Nicole leaves him, whispering 'see you tomorrow', his mood of happiness is shattered by the attack on Pearl Harbour. This shows the impact of this event on the lives of ordinary Americans.

EXAMINER'S TIP: WRITING ABOUT SETTING AND PLACE

Knowledge of the events of the Second World War will give you a better understanding of the issues that Robert Cormier wanted to explore in his novel.

However, the examiner is not looking for you to list historical details. Instead you should concentrate on how the war influenced the themes of the novel and its characters:

● Think about the concept of heroism that the outbreak of war inspires in Frenchtown. How does Cormier try to show the reality that lies behind this concept?

● Think about the way in which the reality of war takes place some distance away from Frenchtown in other parts of the world. What is the effect of this? How do those at home get an impression of the war? How do they come to understand the reality of what happened?

● Cormier said that the inspiration for *Heroes* came from the fiftieth anniversary celebrations for D-day when Allied troops landed on the beaches of northern France, and also from the obituaries in the local paper of the local men and women who fought in the war. Cormier wanted to celebrate the heroism of 'the ordinary people who do their duty quietly, without a fanfare, whether it's fighting a war or going to work every day'.

If you can express your thoughts about issues like these clearly and show the impact they had on the characters in the novel, you will certainly impress the examiner, particularly if you use quotations or examples.

Key themes

Heroism

Heroism is demonstrated in the behaviour of many different characters in a range of ways throughout the novel.

War heroes

- War heroes are portrayed as role models worthy of admiration. The people of Frenchtown are excited by examples of heroism because they do not have to face the consequences of war directly. Heroes represent bravery and patriotism. The people are intensely proud of their very own war hero, Larry LaSalle. Cheers and applause fill the cinema when Larry LaSalle features on the Movietone News after his award of a Silver Star.

- On his return home Larry LaSalle receives a traditional hero's welcome with speeches from the mayor and the whole town turns out to greet him. He is described as a **stereotypical** hero – like a character who has stepped down from the cinema screen, resplendent in his lieutenant's uniform with ribbons and medals on his chest. The young Francis admires Larry for his traditional war exploits, just as he has admired all the young men when they returned home in their uniform.

- Francis and Larry, who were both awarded the Silver Star, are the most obvious representations of heroism but other characters are heroes in their own ways. Robert Cormier uses Arthur Rivier as the representative of ordinary heroes in Chapter 8. Perhaps it is the ordinary heroes that Cormier wants the reader to remember most. We must not forget that the young Germans Francis shot were also heroes to someone too.

Respect for heroes

The novel presents heroes as victims. Their heroism does not bring them happiness.

- Mrs Belander's face 'softened' and she calls him 'poor boy' when she meets Francis because of his injuries.

- In the St Jude Club heroes are treated with the utmost respect. When talking about Larry LaSalle, the bartender's voice becomes 'formal and dignified' (p. 41). He has a scrapbook containing their exploits but he can also see the reality of heroism in front of him.

- Arthur Rivier is surprised that Francis, a war hero with a Silver Star, should wish to remain anonymous, but it is this same respect for Francis which makes him agree to remain silent.

- It is noticeable that Larry welcomes the adulation of others and is happy to be a very public hero.

> **KEY QUOTE**
>
> Francis: 'I was impatient to reach the age when I could join them in that great crusade for freedom' (p. 27).

> **KEY QUOTE**
>
> Francis: 'I could picture him storming a hillside in Guadalcanal, rifle in hand, bayonet fixed, grenades dangling from his belt, pumping bullets into the enemy' (p. 68).

> **KEY QUOTE**
>
> Francis: 'I saw how young they were, boys with apple cheeks, too young to shave. Like me' (p. 24).

EXAMINER'S TIP: WRITING ABOUT THE ILLUSION OF HEROISM

Think about how, in the novel, other people admire heroes but heroes do not seem to admire themselves. As a result, there are different attitudes to heroism in the novel. Perhaps Robert Cormier wants his readers to consider whether Larry LaSalle is an **anti-hero**, someone who may carry out acts of bravery and heroism but also has unattractive and destructive qualities. Should a person like that be regarded as a hero?

HEROES OR ANTI-HEROES?

- Initially Larry is presented as an inspirational figure because of the work he does in the Wreck Centre. He is admired for the way he develops the talents of all who go there.

- It is **ironic** that on the very night he is acclaimed by the whole town for his heroism he destroys the lives of both Francis and Nicole, two young people who regarded him as a hero. But as Larry himself asks, does this flaw in his character destroy all the good he has done?

- Francis himself does not see himself as a hero because of his hidden motive for joining up. In fact he hates to be acclaimed a hero whether by his friend Enrico in Chapter 1, Sister Mathilde and Nicole in Chapters 15 and 16 or even Larry LaSalle in Chapter 14. In that conversation he admits that he was 'a fake all along' (p. 88). However, we can see that he has the courage to challenge Larry and has every intention of killing him in order to expiate his guilt.

EXAMINER'S TIP: WRITING ABOUT THE NATURE OF HEROISM

The theme of heroism runs through the whole of the book. But the nature of heroism remains unclear. Is Francis the character who shows real heroism? Is it Larry? Or Nicole? Or is it Enrico? Or Arthur? Nowhere in the book does any character find comfort or happiness in their heroism. Think about how Cormier's presents the nature of heroism – does it make the book a pessimistic one, or just a realistic one?

REVISION ACTIVITY

- When you have read the book you will be aware that there are many different titles Cormier could have given to his work. Try listing alternative titles as they occur to you.

- Cormier chose the word 'Heroes'. Consider why he chose that as his title for this novel above all other alternatives. Clearly the word and its meanings were more important than any other. So why did he chose it? What was he trying to say?

CONFRONTING EVIL

One of the things that motivates the **characters** to go to war is to confront evil. Yet evil has different forms. There is the external evil that the inhabitants of Frenchtown can all see in their wartime enemy but there is also the evil within their town which they cannot see until it is too late. Not only that, but the enemy soldiers are shown to be young boys just like any other who cry out for their mother when they are killed.

Consequently, evil in the novel is not always obvious:

- Initially Larry LaSalle is worthy of admiration.
- For this reason the revelation of his evil side in the attack on Nicole shocks Francis because it is so unexpected.
- Francis is further shocked in Chapter 14 when Larry reveals that he has always been attracted to 'sweet young things' (p. 90), an attraction which Larry himself considers evil.

Throughout the novel Francis struggles against evil. He believes that his cowardice has resulted in the suffering of the person he loves most and that an act of evil took place because he stood by and did nothing to stop it. For him, the greatest evil occurred where he least expected to find it.

- It is **ironic** that Francis does not carry out his mission to kill Larry, as Larry commits suicide.
- However, in his confrontation with Larry, Francis challenges him for the evil he has done.
- Once Francis has exposed the evil side of his nature, Larry may feel he has no option but to commit suicide.

REVISION ACTIVITY

Look carefully at Chapter 14 where Francis confronts Larry.

- Examine Francis's reactions to Larry and how they develop.
- Notice how he reacts to what Larry says.
- Why doesn't he shoot Larry?
- Why does Larry shoot himself?

GUILT

Francis is consumed by guilt throughout the novel:

- He feels guilt at the thought that he intends to commit murder. His failure to save Nicole from Larry is an even greater source of guilt.
- Francis's sense of guilt is compounded by the guilt he feels at being acclaimed as a hero when he knows he only committed his act of bravery in the hope that he would be killed.

KEY QUOTE

'We love the thing that makes us evil' (p. 76).

★ GRADE BOOSTER

Make a list of events in the novel which you could use when writing about a particular theme so you will have examples ready in your mind when writing an exam answer.

KEY CONNECTION

In *The Chocolate War* by Robert Cormier the central character struggles alone against the corruption in his school and against the school bullies.

KEY CONNECTION

Francis is a character plagued by guilt. In Shakespeare's play, *Hamlet*, the hero suffers from guilt at his inability to avenge his father's murder.

Unlike Francis, Larry does not appear to be troubled by a guilty conscience:

- In Chapter 14 (pp. 90–1) he explains that in his view everyone sins and one sin should not be allowed to wipe away all the good things a person has done.

- He regards his desire for young girls as merely a flaw in his nature. He regrets only that Francis and Nicole no longer see him as the hero they once did.

- Cormier's portrayal of Larry is a complex one and we could argue that his depression at the end of the novel comes more from self-pity than guilt.

FORGIVENESS

The theme of forgiveness is introduced in Chapter 1 where readers see Francis praying for a man who has done him harm. The religious element of forgiveness is emphasised here and again in Chapter 12 where Francis hides in the confessional at St Jude's Church. It is as though he wants immediate forgiveness for his perceived sin of abandoning Nicole when she needed him most.

It appears to be easy for Larry to forgive himself as he does not seem to experience the sense of guilt that Francis does. For Francis self-forgiveness is harder to achieve.

Nicole is the character in the novel who personifies goodness:

- Her first words to Francis are ones of forgiveness, apologising to him for the words she said to him after the attack.

- It is not clear whether her words relieve Francis from his burden of guilt.

- Although she forgives him, it is clear Nicole cannot forget and that she and Francis cannot be friends.

? DID YOU KNOW

Robert Cormier, when discussing the theme of guilt in his novels, said, 'God is always there to forgive you, but it's harder forgiving yourself.'

LONELINESS

Many of the **characters** in the novel appear to live alone, separated from their past. They often struggle to communicate their real feelings and withdraw into themselves.

- At the end of the novel Nicole is alone in the convent far away from the friends she made in Frenchtown. She tries to cut herself off from her past.

- Although for the greater part of the novel Larry is surrounded by crowds of people, at the end he is seen as a sad and lonely figure in his lodgings.

- Francis chooses loneliness, refusing to reveal himself to people he knows.

- Arthur Rivier wanders the streets at night, drunk and alone.

- The loneliness of characters is often linked to the secrets they carry within them. It is their secret or hidden identity which sets them apart from others.

When he walks the streets of Frenchtown, Francis remains hidden behind his scarf, a visible sign of his separation from his past. He embraces loneliness because he is ashamed of his identity. Even when he is in a crowded place he is still alone, not taking part in the action but merely observing. This also reflects his childhood experiences as a lonely child brought up by his uncle.

EXAMINER'S TIP: WRITING ABOUT THE SENSE OF ISOLATION THAT THE CHARACTERS EXPERIENCE

Examine the way in which the characters struggle to communicate effectively:

- Nicole's reaction to the assault is to run away, taking her pain with her. The few words she exchanges with Francis before she leaves add to his state of despair.

- Francis can only return to Frenchtown as a stranger, since he is filled with self-loathing as a result of what he sees as his failure. He hates who he is so he needs to become someone else, hiding from the people he once knew.

- Larry returns to Frenchtown but now he is no longer surrounded by admirers. He too can never recapture the past and lives alone, sitting in a rocking chair, not playing table tennis or dancing as before.

- Arthur feels trapped because he cannot speak to anyone about the war and feels no one cares about what he experienced.

REVISION ACTIVITY

Think about the loneliness of Francis and his lack of engagement with others on his return to Frenchtown.

- What advantages does this give to Robert Cormier?
- How does he use this as a device in the novel?

Look especially at the chapters which are not set in the past: Chapters 1, 4, 6, 8, 10 and 13.

? DID YOU KNOW

Robert Cormier once said, 'I have always had the sense that we are all pretty much alone in life, particularly in adolescence.'

KEY QUOTE

Francis: 'The visit to Nicole's house on Sixth Street brought back only loneliness and regret' (p. 26).

KEY CONNECTION

Read *I Am the Cheese* by Robert Cormier which is based around the theme of hidden identity.

APPEARANCE AND REALITY

When Sister Mathilde says to Francis 'We all have secrets' (p. 95), she is in fact talking about everyone in the novel. There is a difference between how characters present themselves and the reality which lies beneath.

● In the veterans' club Arthur Rivier hides his depression after the war.

● Enrico Rucelli hides his despair behind a mask of humorous remarks.

● Francis goes to great lengths to hide his identity on his return to Frenchtown.

● The theme of hidden identity is exemplified in the character of Larry LaSalle, about whom there have been rumours since his first appearance in Frenchtown.

● Nicole hides the attack from her family in order to spare them pain.

Of course the difference between the appearance and reality of war is the central part of Robert Cormier's novel. The people in Frenchtown see a sanitised version of glory and heroism in the cinema. They are proud of the contribution they can make to a war which is taking place such a long way away. However, the survivors bring back with them the reality of their wartime experiences.

EXAMINER'S TIP: WRITING ABOUT FRANCIS'S DISGUISE

The white silk scarf and the Red Sox cap that Francis wears serve not only to protect people from being distressed by his terrible injuries, but also to prevent them from recognising him. His desire to avoid recognition has a practical purpose as he does not wish to be recognised before he kills Larry LaSalle.

However, his disguise is also a **symbol** of his shame, the shame that he carries everywhere with him and which haunts his waking hours – the shame of being recognised as a war hero, a bearer of the Silver Star, when actually his act of bravery was motivated by the selfish desire to be killed.

There is an **irony** in the novel in that readers are aware of Francis's hidden identity from the start while characters whom he meets such as Arthur Rivier or Mrs Belander are not, thus creating suspense. This also enables the reader to sympathise with Francis during the moments when he fears recognition, such as when he is looking for lodgings or making his first appearance in the St Jude Club.

REVISION ACTIVITY

Look at the three main characters, Francis, Larry and Nicole. They have different motives for hiding their secrets or their identities.

Divide a piece of paper into three columns and write down each of their reasons.

Notice how Francis, Larry and Nicole have one thing in common: the terrible event in the Wreck Centre. It is ironic that the secret that they share is responsible for dividing them.

Progress and revision check

REVISION ACTIVITY

Who says these things in the novel? (Write your answers below)

1. 'No heroes in that scrap-book, Francis. Only us, the boys of Frenchtown.'

   ....

2. 'I know what he was. For a while there he made me feel special.'

   ....

3. 'Your secret is safe with me.'

   ....

4. 'Leave everything here, the war, what happened at the Wreck Centre.'

   ....

5. 'My hero from the war.'

   ....

REVISION ACTIVITY

On a piece of paper write down answers to these questions:

● How does Francis's childhood shape the person he becomes?

  Start: *We are aware that Francis is a lonely child who finds it difficult to make friends. He prefers to spend his time reading. In fact he tells Nicole that his ambition is to read every book in the library …*

● How does Robert Cormier explore the concept of evil in the novel?

  Start: *The presentation of evil is complicated. When war breaks out everyone believes that they know where the evil is that they need to confront but …*

GRADE BOOSTER

Answer this longer practice question about a theme in the novel:

Q: How does Robert Cormier deal with the theme of loyalty in *Heroes*?

For a C grade: show how the idea of loyalty runs through the book. Francis is loyal to his comrades in the war and shows great loyalty and commitment to Nicole. Indicate that he does not believe he is worthy of loyalty in return. Other characters have their own brand of loyalty, to their country, which is clearly displayed in their reactions to the outbreak of war. Show how their experiences in the war create a real sense of loyalty and mutual respect on their return.

For an A grade: deal with all the issues above but expand the answer to examine the difficulties faced when making a judgement about Larry. His loyalty is entirely to himself. Show how the loyalty and respect the others have for him is at first exploited and then betrayed. Also mention that the friendship Marie shows and the supportive comments Nicole makes to Francis about his future show that loyalty is an essential human quality. Use appropriate quotations to support your answer.

Language

Here are some useful terms to know when writing about *Heroes*, what they mean and how they appear in the novel.

Literary term	Means?	Example
Juxtaposition	The placing of words or ideas side by side or consecutively to highlight the differences between them.	After stating that Nicole made his visits to the Wreck Centre complete, Robert Cormier introduces Joey LeBlanc's references to doom. 'Doom,' he pronounced. 'Wait and see' (p. 37).
Metaphor	An image which describes something as if it were something else.	After the rape, Nicole's face is seen in a 'slash of moonlight' (p. 75). This emphasises the violence she has experienced.
Simile	When one thing is said to be like another, using 'as' or 'like'.	Francis describes the two German soldiers appearing 'like grim ghosts' (p. 23), which emphasises how their deaths will haunt him forever.
Symbolism	An object which represents something else.	Francis's duffel bag which he carries everywhere represents his feeling of guilt.
Pathetic fallacy	Using nature to express human feelings.	Cormier uses the weather – rain, low clouds and stifling heat – to reflect Francis's depression and the intense despair he feels.
Irony	When one meaning is expected but the opposite is true.	The title of the novel itself is ironic as characters who are regarded as heroes such as Francis and Larry do not always behave in heroic ways.

REVISION ACTIVITY

Try making your own version of the table above. Use the **Literary terms** at the back of these **York Notes** and supply your own examples from the novel.

EXAMINER'S TIP: WRITING ABOUT IRONY

Irony is an important part of Robert Cormier's work since the title of the novel itself is ironic. Cormier uses **irony** to suggest that there is more than one interpretation, e.g. characters who are regarded as heroes do not always behave in heroic ways. Is Larry a hero? Or Francis?

● Francis views himself as a coward because he claims that he carried out a heroic deed accidentally in an attempt to kill himself. This itself is ironic.

● The **irony** of the name of the 'Wreck' Centre is clear as the lives of Francis and Nicole are wrecked as a result of what happened there.

● Words and phrases have an ironic meaning when interpreted in the light of later events. This is particularly true in the case of Larry LaSalle. When we read 'he manipulated a spotlight' (p. 47) for Nicole this takes on a sinister meaning as we realise that he also manipulated her affections. Larry's slender figure is described as 'lethal' (p. 68) at the beginning of Chapter 11. Does this give readers a hint that by the end of the chapter his behaviour will be lethal too?

DESCRIPTIVE LANGUAGE

One feature of Cormier's style is that he can create realistic descriptions of people and places by the use of a few well-chosen details. These details often match the mood of the characters, or provide a suggestion of things to come. Here are some examples:

● The bleakness of Francis's life is matched by the description of his damp cold lodgings in Chapter 3 (p. 21).

● When the Wreck Centre was completed it still looked unfinished: 'The white paint didn't completely cover the dark patches of mildew on the clapboards and the shutters sagged next to the windows' (p. 32). This suggestion of imperfection and decay fits well with the events which are to take place there.

● There is a very detailed description of Francis's war experience in the French village which contains references to the five senses. This enables readers to picture the scene as Robert Cormier refers to sights such as 'late afternoon shadows' and sounds such as 'sudden gunfire ... quiet curses floating on the air' (pp. 22–3).

● Later, the joyfulness of celebrations for Larry's return is captured in the account of the women's dresses: 'glittery sequins catching the light from a crystal ball' (p. 70).

● In the veterans' club the change of mood from jovial to melancholic is conveyed by a description of the veterans such as George Richelieu 'tugging at his pinned-up sleeve which should hold his arm' or Armand who 'stares off into space, looking at something nobody else can see' (p. 40).

EXAMINER'S TIP

If you want to do well in the examination, you should organise your revision notes carefully. Try using different colour dividers for different sections of your notes.

? DID YOU KNOW

The feast day of St Jude is 28 October. He is regarded as the patron saint of Desperate Cases and Hopeless Causes. Do you think this has any significance? Why did Robert Cormier decide to call the church by this name rather than by another?

KEY QUOTE

The horror of the final words of the opening sentence, 'the war is over and I have no face' (p. 1) seems more shocking because of the use of the first-person pronoun.

RELIGIOUS LANGUAGE

Guilt and forgiveness are themes which are embedded in the novel, and supported by the frequent use of religious vocabulary.

● When Francis first prays in St Jude's Church he refers to the 'odours of forgiveness' (p. 6).

● Nicole reminds Francis of the statue of St Thérèse, 'in the niche next to Father Balthazar's confessional' (p. 10).

● The smell of ashes after Francis has burned the address and telephone number of Dr Abrams is compared to incense.

● When Francis speaks to Nicole after the attack he stands before her 'as if all my sins had been revealed' (p. 80).

● Even Larry LaSalle, who does not appear to have a conscience, refers to his sins. 'Everybody sins, Francis. The terrible thing is we love our sins' (p. 90).

THE LANGUAGE STYLE USED BY ROBERT CORMIER

● Short sentences and simple vocabulary are characteristic features of the style of *Heroes*. These are linked to the **narrative voice** of Francis Cassavant and allow us to feel as though he is speaking to us directly, allowing us to listen to his thoughts. As a result, his detailed and at times brutal description of the injuries he received has great impact.

● In spite of his severe injuries, Francis Cassavant is not portrayed as self-pitying. For example, after he has stated that people often cross the street when they see him coming, he simply comments: 'I don't blame them' (p. 3).

● Sometimes the thoughts of Francis Cassavant are recorded in italics as if they are part of the **dialogue**. When Nicole tells him she is fine Francis thinks to himself: *'You don't sound fine'* (p. 99).

● The simplicity of the opening paragraph of the novel ending with the direct statement 'I have no face' (p. 1) both shocks readers and compels them to read on. Such language creates tension and suspense.

● Sometimes the short sharp sentences are emphasised by their arrangement on separate lines. After Francis has finally discovered the whereabouts of Larry LaSalle in Chapter 13, three short direct sentences complete the chapter, finishing with 'And I know where to find him' (p. 84).

● The voices of the other characters in the novel are reflected in the dialogue. The short conversation between Arthur Rivier and Francis reveals the respect Arthur has for a veteran with terrible injuries such as Francis: 'Land mine? … Grenade then? … Tough … tough …' (p. 26). The briefness of their words suggests their shared experience.

● Nicole's affection for Francis and her own sweet nature can be detected in her final conversation with him: 'My good Francis. My table tennis champion. My Silver Star hero' (p. 103), the word 'my' emphasising her affection for him.

EXAMINER'S TIP: WRITING ABOUT FRANCIS AS NARRATOR

Everything that happens in the novel is recounted from the point of view of the main **protagonist**, Francis Cassavant. As a result we identify closely with his thoughts and feelings as he moves around Frenchtown in search of Larry LaSalle.

The **first-person narration** enables the reader to sympathise more closely with Francis, particularly at times when he describes himself as an outsider – 'alone on the back steps of the Wreck Centre' (p. 43) – or contemplates suicide at the top of St Jude's church tower (p. 81).

KEY CONNECTION

All Quiet on the Western Front, a novel about the First World War, is written in the first person and views the war through the eyes of a young German recruit.

Structure

USE OF FLASHBACKS

The structure of the novel expands our understanding of the **characters** and the experiences that have shaped them.

Here are some key points to bear in mind:

- *Heroes* does not follow a straightforward **chronological narrative**. The narrative moves from present to past, with the result that the readers are able to build up a fuller picture of the lives of the main **protagonists**, Francis Cassavant, Nicole Renard and Larry LaSalle.

- The flashbacks are necessary because they show how each of the characters has changed and developed throughout their lives.

- The frequently changing flashbacks could also be seen to represent the different sides of Francis's character. His personality has many different aspects to it; he is at times light-hearted and at others deeply depressed. On occasions he is troubled by guilt, unable to take positive action. The divisions in his character and his varying moods throughout the novel are reflected in the structure of the novel.

- The flashbacks take place in the first twelve chapters. This establishes the behaviour and the motivation of the characters.

- All the events of the past build up to Francis's confrontation with Larry in Chapter 14. At the same time, suspense is created in the novel by the use of flashbacks as they slow the action down. Details are revealed gradually.

KEY QUOTE

Francis: 'At that moment, I knew that I was really anonymous, that I wasn't Francis Joseph Cassavant anymore but a tenant in Frenchtown' (p. 5).

REVISION ACTIVITY

Overleaf are the key flashbacks as they appear in the novel.

Try numbering these in order of importance. Which of these nine episodes has the most impact on the outcome of the novel – and why?

- Chapter 1: a conversation with Enrico Rucelli in hospital.
- Chapter 2: Francis's first meeting with Nicole at school.
- Chapter 3: the attack on the French village where Francis received his injuries.
- Chapter 5: the opening of the Wreck Centre.
- Chapter 7: the table tennis match at the Wreck Centre.
- Chapter 9: Larry's departure for the war, and the affection between Francis and Nicole.
- Chapter 10: Francis's time in England and his discovery of the nature of his injuries.
- Chapter 11: Larry's return from the war and his attack on Nicole.
- Chapter 12: Francis's conversation with Nicole after the attack and his suicidal thoughts.

Progress and revision check

REVISION ACTIVITY

1. How is Larry's dancing style described in Chapter 5? (Write your answers below)

....

2. What important flashback are we shown in Chapter 3?

....

3. Who gave Francis the white silk scarf that he wears?

....

4. Why is the hot weather in Frenchtown after the assault on Nicole an appropriate image?

....

5. How is the positive mood at the end of the table tennis competition suddenly destroyed?

....

REVISION ACTIVITY

On a piece of paper write down answers to these questions:

● Why is the white silk scarf an important **symbol** in the novel?

Start: *The scarf reminds Francis of those worn by First World War aviators. To him this symbolises heroism which is ironic because …*

● Why is it important that Francis sees himself as a knight at Nicole's feet when he first meets her?

Start: *This is an important simile because it emphasises how Francis sees Nicole. To him she becomes a symbol of …*

GRADE BOOSTER

Answer this longer practice question about the narrative structure of the novel:

Q: How does the way that the novel is structured add to our understanding of the characters in *Heroes*?

For a C grade: show how the plot is a very simple sequence of events. Then show how Robert Cormier develops the plot through the use of flashbacks. Indicate that he explains events in the past which have influenced the central characters and made them what they are in the present. Show how the use of Francis as a narrator makes us sympathise with him.

For an A grade: as well as developing the above you need to indicate that Robert Cormier increases our understanding of events through other techniques. The use of Francis as a narrator opens up his thoughts for us to see. He exposes his emotions which gives the book great power. Show how the author creates tension around the character of Larry by indicating from the start that Francis wants to kill him. This influences the way in which we respond to his character.

PART SIX: GRADE BOOSTER

Understanding the question

Questions in examinations or controlled conditions often need 'decoding'. Decoding the question helps to ensure that your answer will be relevant and refers to what you have been asked.

 UNDERSTAND EXAM LANGUAGE

Get used to exam and essay style language by looking at specimen questions and the words they use. For example:

Exam speak!	Means?	Example
'convey ideas'	'get across a point to the reader'. Usually you have to say how this is done.	The way Cormier describes Francis's injuries conveys the horrible reality of war.
'methods, techniques, ways'	The 'things' the writer does – such as a powerful description, introducing a shocking event, how someone speaks.	The description of the murder of Marie Blanche establishes the atmosphere which surrounds the Wreck Centre.
'present, represent'	1) present: 'the way in which things are told to us' 2) represent: 'what those things might mean underneath'	The writer presents the reader with descriptions of the people of Frenchtown's reaction to the outbreak of war, representing their patriotism and their support of the young people who fight for their country.

 'BREAK DOWN' THE QUESTION

Pick out the **key words** or phrases. For example:

> **Question:** How does Robert Cormier use the **character of Francis** to **explore** the **idea of loneliness** in the novel?

- The focus is on **character** (Francis Cassavant) so you will need to talk about him, what he does and how he presents himself and how others react to him.

- The reference to '**explore** the **idea of loneliness**' indicates that this is a question about one of the themes in the novel, e.g. the loneliness that Francis experiences both before and after the war.

What does this tell you? **Focus** on Francis and show how his childhood is often solitary and how after the war he isolates himself from contact with others.

 KNOW YOUR LITERARY LANGUAGE!

When studying texts you will come across words such as 'theme', 'symbol', 'imagery', 'metaphor', etc. Some of these words could come up in the question you are asked. Make sure you know what they mean before you use them!

Planning your answer

It is vital that you **plan** your response to the controlled assessment task or possible exam question carefully, and then follow your plan, if you are to gain higher grades.

 DO THE RESEARCH!

When revising for the exam, or planning your response to the controlled assessment task, collect **evidence** (for example, quotations) that will support what you have to say. For example, if preparing to answer a question on the way Robert Cormier allows us to see the different sides of Larry LaSalle's character, you might list ideas as follows:

Key point	Evidence/quotation	Page/chapter. etc
Larry is very supportive of Francis and ensures that he wins the table tennis competition to boost his confidence.	Francis tells us 'I realized that he was letting me win, was guiding the game with such skill that no one but me realized what he was doing.'	Chapter 7, p. 52

 PLAN FOR PARAGRAPHS

Use paragraphs to plan your answer. For example:

1 The first paragraph should **introduce** the **argument** you wish to make.
2 Then, jot down how the paragraphs that follow will **develop** this argument. Include **details**, **examples** and other possible **points of view**.
3 **Sum up** your argument in the last paragraph.

For example, for the following task:

Question: How does Cormier present the character of Nicole?

- Paragraph 1: *Introduction*, Nicole is important because of the effect she has on Francis and because she provides the link between the two male characters.

- Paragraph 2: *First point*, e.g. Nicole's importance is emphasised in her first appearance. Use of religious images shows that she is a symbol of purity.

- Paragraph 3: *Second point*, e.g. Cormier establishes the goodness of her character. She enjoys Francis's company, she encourages him. She has a playful teasing attitude towards him. She shares her dreams for the future with him.

- Paragraph 4: *Third point*, e.g. Nicole is shown to be attractive and also innocent. She enjoys the attention and status she gets from Larry but doesn't understand his motives. Refer to the dancing and her use of his Christian name.

- Paragraph 5: *Fourth point*, e.g. After the attack she blames Francis. She is angry. She later regrets this, which shows her good nature, but the attack has changed her, as symbolised by the writer's description of her cut hair.

- Paragraph 6: *Conclusion*, e.g. Sum up the character of Nicole.

How to use quotations

One of the secrets of success in writing essays is to use quotations **effectively**. There are five basic principles:

❶ Put quotation marks, e.g. ' ' around the quotation.
❷ Write the quotation exactly as it appears in the original.
❸ Do not use a quotation that repeats what you have just written.
❹ Use the quotation so that it fits into your sentence, or if it is longer indent it as a separate paragraph.
❺ Only quote what is most useful.

 USE QUOTATIONS TO DEVELOP YOUR ARGUMENT

Quotations should be used to develop the line of thought in your essays. Your comment should not duplicate what is in your quotation. Compare these two examples:

GRADE D/E   GRADE C

(simply repeats the idea)	(makes a point, supports it with a relevant quotation, explains idea)
The young people of Frenchtown regarded Larry LaSalle as their champion and enjoyed being with him, 'He was our champion and we were happy to be in his presence' (p. 35).	The young people of Frenchtown thought highly of Larry LaSalle, describing how 'he was our champion and we were happy to be in his presence' (p. 35), suggesting he was admired by all.

However, the most sophisticated way of using the writer's words is to embed them into your sentence, and further develop the point:

GRADE A

(makes point, embeds quote, develops idea, zooming in on key words/phrases)
The young people of Frenchtown thought highly of Larry LaSalle, calling him their 'champion', and were 'happy to be in his presence' (p. 29), suggesting both his charisma and approachability. 'Champion', in particular, links to the idea of heroism and physical prowess, which is later questioned in the text.

When you use quotations in this way, you are demonstrating the ability to use text as evidence to support your ideas – not simply including words from the original to prove you have read it.

EXAMINER'S TIP

Where relevant, aim to include examples of contrasting moods in the novel to show you have a good grasp of the writer's style.

GRADE BOOSTER

As part of your exam preparation, make a list of three or four quotations for each character taken from different stages of the novel.

Sitting the examination

Examination papers are carefully designed to give you the opportunity to do your best. Follow these handy hints for exam success.

 BEFORE YOU START

- Make sure that you **know the texts** you are writing about so that you are properly prepared and equipped.

- You need to be **comfortable** and **free from distractions**. Inform the invigilator if anything is off-putting, e.g. a shaky desk.

- **Read** and follow the instructions, or rubric, on the front of the examination paper. You should know by now what you need to do but **check** to reassure yourself.

- Before beginning your answer have a **skim** through the **whole paper** to make sure you don't miss anything **important**.

- Observe the **time allocation** – and follow it carefully. If they recommend 45 minutes for a particular question on a text, make sure this is how long you spend.

 WRITING YOUR RESPONSES

A typical 40 minute examination essay is probably between 500 and 750 words in length.

Ideally, spend 3–4 minutes planning your answer before you begin.

Use the questions to structure your response. Here is an example:

Question: Do you regard the ending of the novel as hopeful or negative? What details and methods does Robert Cormier use to lead you to this view?

- The introduction to your answer could briefly describe **the ending** of the novel.

- The second part could explain how the ending offers the reader some **hope**.

- The third part could be an exploration of the **negative** aspects.

- The conclusion would **sum up your own viewpoint**.

For each part allocate paragraphs to cover the points you wish to make (see **Planning your answer**).

Keep your writing clear and easy to read, using paragraphs and link words to show the structure of your answers.

Spend a couple of minutes afterwards quickly checking for obvious errors.

 'KEY WORDS' ARE THE KEY!

Keep on mentioning the **key words** from the question in your answer. This will keep you on track and remind the examiner that you are answering the question set.

🔓 **EXAMINER'S TIP**

Take highlighters into the exam to highlight key words in the questions but do not use them to highlight anything in your answer.

🔓 **EXAMINER'S TIP**

Writing a plan for longer exam essays helps you to focus on the question and improve your mark.

 **GRADE BOOSTER**

Aim to refer to the title of the question in your introduction. Remember to keep your introduction short.

Responding to a passage from the text

It may be the case that you are asked to answer a question or questions on a **short passage** from *Heroes* in the exam. Follow these useful tips for success.

 ## WHAT YOU ARE REQUIRED TO DO

Make sure you are clear about:

● The **specific passage you have been given** and the **question(s)** related to it (check that the question you answer is the one about the passage!).

● How **long** you have to write your answer (i.e. 20 minutes?).

● The **sort of question** you have been asked; it is likely to be one in which you have to **show how** the **writer** gets something **across to the reader** (e.g., the techniques and language Cormier uses to reveal character, setting, theme, etc.).

 **EXAMINER'S TIP**

The question you have been given will almost certainly be about the writer's use of language and how effects are created. Keep referring to the writer, i.e. 'The writer shows how ...', 'The writer conveys through imagery ...', etc.

 ## HOW YOU CAN PREPARE

It might seem that it is difficult to prepare for an 'unseen' passage but you can:

● Select any passage from *Heroes* of about 300 words. Practise skim reading it quickly and then making notes on:

  ❶ what you learn from the passage,

  ❷ the effect of the language used by the writer.

● Practise writing a 20-minute answer based on one of the **Further Questions** at the back of these **York Notes**.

● Use these **York Notes** to check key passages or chapters, reread what makes them important and how the writer creates specific effects.

 **GRADE BOOSTER**

Don't waste time retelling what happens in the passage. Your focus must be on the language used and what it tells us.

 ## DURING THE EXAM

Remember:

● **Stick** to the passage and question you have been given. You only have 20 minutes so don't be diverted into other areas.

● Don't panic about **having time** to **read** an 'unseen' passage. The chances are you will **know** the passage or have **already read it** in class or at home.

● The allocated **time** is for **reading** and **writing**, so make the most of it. You won't have time to plan, so quickly read the text and get started!

● The question will expect you to make **close reference** to the given text. This means you should quote **well-chosen words** and **phrases** from the passage in your answer.

● Keep your quotations **short** and **relevant** to the question.

Improve your grade

It is useful to know the type of responses examiners are looking for when they award different grades. The following broad guidance should help you to improve your grade when responding to the questions you are set!

GRADE C

What you need to show	What this means
Personal, sustained response to task and text	You write enough! You don't run out of ideas after two paragraphs.
Effective use of **textual details** to **support your explanations**	You generally support what you say with evidence, e.g. *The effects of war can be seen throughout the book. In the first chapter there is a detailed description of Francis's injuries and in the last chapter we see the ordinary soldiers who are the 'real heroes of the war'.*
Explanation of the writer's **use of language, structure, form**, etc., and the **effect on readers**	You must write about the writer's use of these things. It's not enough simply to give a viewpoint. So, you might comment on how **contrasts** are used. For example, when we last see Larry in a flashback he is moving among the young people, playing table tennis and dancing. When we next see him in the present he is confined to his chair in a rented room.
Convey ideas clearly and **appropriately**	What you say is relevant and is easy for the examiner to follow. If the task asks you to comment on how Larry is presented, that is who you write about.

GRADE A

What you need to show in addition to the above	What this means
Ability to **speculate** about the text and **explore alternative** responses	You look beyond the obvious. You might question the idea of Nicole's goodness – is her rejection of Francis to blame for later events?
Close analysis and apt selection of **textual detail**	If you are looking at Cormier's use of language, you carefully select and comment on each word in a line or phrase drawing out its distinctive effect on the reader, e.g. *When Joey says that he can still feel a sense of doom hanging over the Wreck Centre at the end of Chapter 5, we are aware that Cormier has deliberately used the word 'wreck' instead of 'Rec.' The anger of Francis when he slams the door indicates how important meeting Nicole there has become for him. It is significant that Cormier allows Joey to have the last word.*
Convincing and **imaginative interpretation**	Your viewpoint is likely to convince the examiner. You show you have *engaged* with the text, and come up with your own ideas, but you have also sustained your argument across your essay, drawing on a wide range of aspects and evidence.

Annotated sample answers

This section will provide you with **extracts** from two **model answers**, one at **C grade** and one at **A grade**, to give you an idea of what is required to achieve different levels.

> **Question:** How does Cormier make the reader aware of the different effects of war on people's lives?

CANDIDATE 1

This comment isn't needed since it is not strictly relevant

Repeats the same point in a different way

Name Joey LeBlanc here

Good quotation

Heroes is a novel by Robert Cormier which deals with the war. The war affects the lives of many people in the novel including Francis Cassavant. At the beginning of the novel he describes how he lost his face in a grenade attack. He did not want to recover because he had hoped he would die in the war. This means that for the rest of his life he feels a failure.

The writer intends to show that there are some positive effects of war. At first there is excitement in Frenchtown as men and women follow Larry's example and join up. There is pride and patriotism as they watch him on the Movietone News. Francis originally wanted to fight in the war. In Chapter 4 he refers to soldiers like Arthur Rivier, saying 'I was impatient to reach the age when I could join them in that great crusade for freedom.' They think that the war is a great adventure.

Those who remain in Frenchtown form their impressions of the war from the cinema especially when they watch Larry. They do not experience war like the soldiers do. The soldiers' impressions are very different. They see death and suffering at first hand. They cannot escape their memories. Some die and others bring the war home with them.

Cormier uses powerful language in Chapter 3 when Francis relives his war experiences. He makes war seem brutal when he writes about Francis killing a German soldier: 'the head of one of the soldiers exploded like a ripe tomato'. He shows the cruelty of war when he writes about one of the German soldiers with 'apple cheeks, too young to shave'. He tells us that one of the soldiers cried out 'Mama' as he died, which makes us feel sympathetic and shows us that there is no difference between the two sides.

Perhaps the word 'hero' could be used here

Good link

Link the quotation with Francis and his face

Good – develop this point in more detail

> **Overall comment:** The points made are mostly relevant and appropriate to the question. The student has used textual details effectively to support a clearly expressed argument. There are some areas for development – the essay would have been strengthened by the inclusion of Enrico and an exploration of the psychological impact of the war displayed by Arthur, and quotations could be analysed in more depth.

GRADE C

CANDIDATE 2

A good start linking the beginning and the end of the novel

The theme of war permeates the whole novel. From the opening chapter with its horrific description of the war injuries sustained by Francis Cassavant right to the final chapter where he thinks about the ordinary soldiers who are the 'real heroes of the war', no character in the novel remains untouched by war. The writer's purpose is to make readers very aware of the devastating effects of war, and also to show that the idea of war can be glamorous.

Independent and original thinking

Interesting reflections on community reactions

Cormier does not always present war as a negative force with regard to its effects on people. The war effort unites the people of Frenchtown, bringing them out of their houses to discuss the war at Laurier's drugstore or to watch the exploits of their town's war heroes on the cinema screen. Larry's homecoming is celebrated with a great deal of patriotism; his reward for bravery is viewed as an award for the whole town. The same patriotism is seen in the writer's use of vocabulary in Chapter 4 where Francis refers to the war as 'the great crusade for freedom.' At the end of the war, however, we are aware of the consequences on the young people who took part. They inspire sympathy and in Francis's case, horror.

Needs more exploration here

Notice how the physical and the psychological effects of war are linked by his dream

One of Cormier's most powerful descriptions of the horrific effects of war is to be found in Chapter 3 where Francis relives the horror of war in a nightmare sequence. Frequent references to the fear of his fellow soldiers with details such as Henry Johnson's 'ragged breathing' and Eddie Richards's diarrhoea bring home to the reader what the soldiers had to endure. The nightmare aspect of the experience is emphasised in the simile 'like grim ghosts' to describe the sudden appearance of the German soldiers.

The violence of war is brought out in another simile in which a soldier's 'head exploded like a ripe tomato' giving readers a very graphic image of the loss of a young life. The poignancy of the loss of young men in the war is highlighted in the description of the soldiers Francis killed: 'boys with apple cheeks, too young to shave', the use of 'apple' implying both goodness and health. The irony of war, that young men from one country are destroying the lives of young men from another, is brought home to readers with Francis's comment: 'like me'.

Quote is embedded and an apt example of literary device

Appropriate use of a language term

Good point but perhaps needs a stronger conclusion.

It is no accident that the novel ends with Francis reflecting on his comrades in the war. To him they were 'scared kids, not born to fight and kill'.

Overall comment: This is a confident answer, showing analysis and personal engagement with the text. There is a good range of reference and the inclusion of minor characters is impressive. There are good links between paragraphs and there is a clear sequence and well-chosen quotations. However, there could have been greater development of the effects of the war on the community. The interesting notion of war as 'glamorous' is not fully pursued, and Joey and Enrico deserve a mention, but overall an excellent response.

GRADE A

Further questions

The following questions are a representative sample of examination questions from all the major examination boards.

EXAM-STYLE QUESTIONS

❶ Look carefully at this quotation, 'Does that one sin of mine wipe away all the good things?' Write about how Robert Cormier presents the character of Larry LaSalle showing how both good and bad aspects of his character are portrayed in the novel.

❷ How does Robert Cormier use the characters of Joey LeBlanc and Arthur Rivier as commentators on the action and themes of the novel?

❸ One of the powerful themes of the novel is that all the characters are damaged in one way or other. Do you agree with this statement?

❹ How does Cormier use the structure of *Heroes* to build suspense and add depth to the story?

❺ What does the novel tell you about bravery and cowardice?

❻ How does Robert Cormier present the themes of guilt and forgiveness in *Heroes*?

QUESTIONS ON SET PASSAGES FROM THE NOVEL

Read the extract that is given, then practise writing your response in 20 minutes.

❶ Read the passage when Nicole is first introduced on p. 10 up to the middle of p. 11.

With close reference to the text show how the writer presents Nicole and what effect is created.

❷ Read pp. 22–4, the flashback sequence.

With close reference to the text show how Cormier presents the reality of war and its effects on those involved.

❸ Read the beginning of Chapter 11 – Larry's homecoming.

With close reference to the text show how Cormier presents Larry here.

Literary terms

Literary term	Explanation
character(s)	Either a person in a play, novel, etc., or his or her personality.
anti-hero	A hero with negative characteristics. For example, Larry LaSalle.
chronological narrative	A story which follows events in the order in which they happened.
dialogue	A conversation between characters.
first-person narration	A story told from the point of view of the narrator, using the personal pronoun 'I'.
irony	Where a character does the opposite of what is expected in a particular situation. For example, when Larry LaSalle kills himself although readers have been expecting Francis to carry out his mission to kill Larry.
juxtaposition	The placing of words or ideas side by side or consecutively to highlight the differences between them. For example, at the end of Chapter 5 after stating that Nicole's presence made Francis's trip to the Wreck Centre complete, Robert Cormier introduces Joey LeBlanc's references to doom.
metaphor	An image which describes something as if it were something else. For example, 'He could tap dance with machine-gun speed' (p. 33).
narrative voice	The storyteller's voice through which events are presented and which gives readers the point of view of the narrator.
protagonist	The central character in a novel or short story, the one around whom the action revolves.
simile	A comparison using 'as' or 'like'. For example, 'a deep sadness settles on me as if winter has invaded my bones' (p. 87).
stereotype	A typical characteristic based on the belief that a particular group of people all share the same characteristics and behaviour. For example, Larry LaSalle is presented as a stereotypical war hero, good looking and courageous.
structural device	The way in which a text is organised by a writer to add meaning. In a novel this could refer to the inclusion of a character designed to give readers information about events or other characters, e.g. Joey LeBlanc.
symbol	An object which represents something else. For example, Francis's duffel bag which he carries everywhere represents his feeling of guilt.

Checkpoint answers

Checkpoint 1

Francis needs the scarf and bandage to hide his identity. He does not want to be recognised as he carries out his mission (p. 2). Perhaps he also wants to avoid being recognised as a hero who has been awarded a Silver Star.

Checkpoint 2

The phrase 'small and slender' suggests Nicole is delicate and possibly in need of protection, while 'shining black hair' suggests she is beautiful. 'The pale purity of her face' implies innocence. Her face reminds Francis of the statue of St Thérèse, giving the impression she is almost saintly. However, the hint of mischief in her eyes suggests another side to her character.

Checkpoint 3

The words of Norman Rocheleau, 'I don't know where they went, the Renards. They left without warning in the middle of the night' (p. 17) create an air of mystery around Nicole and her family.

Checkpoint 4

In Chapter 4, in the St Jude Club, Francis stands apart from the other veterans. He refers to their laughter creating 'a camaraderie in the bar, a fellowship I wish I could be part of' (p. 28).

Checkpoint 5

Cormier gives details of Arthur's baseball achievements for two reasons: to emphasise that there are other types of heroism other than war heroism and to show how the war has changed him.

Checkpoint 6

Francis feels he must remain sharp and alert in case Larry LaSalle should come in or someone mentions his name. He wants to be sure he does not miss anything to do with the possible arrival of Larry LaSalle.

Checkpoint 7

'It's a sport you're going to dominate with your quickness and your reflexes', 'Beautiful' – when Francis returns a difficult spin, 'You're a natural', 'It's what natural athletes have', 'You also have a great return' (pp. 44–5).

Checkpoint 8

When Joey LeBlanc calls out to Larry 'Francis has got your number' (p. 51), he could be suggesting that Francis is aware that Larry is attracted to Nicole and therefore could be a rival to him.

Checkpoint 9

'The sorrow in [Arthur's] voice' (p. 55) suggests that for him the war was a painful experience.

Checkpoint 10

Nicole gives Francis confidence by: talking to him about books, showing she was interested in the same things as he was; accepting his invitation to the cinema and continuing to go out with him; telling him he had the ability to become a writer; and teasing him – 'she had a way of teasing which coaxed me into forgetting my shyness' (p. 60).

Checkpoint 11

By the word 'disposal' Francis means his own suicide. He wants to commit suicide because there is nothing else in life to motivate him after the killing of Larry LaSalle. He may wish to die as an act of despair because he has betrayed Nicole, the person he loved.

Checkpoint 12

Francis feels bitter at this point because he is in a state of shock having seen his horrific injuries for the first time. The doctors and nurses had not prepared him for the fact that he had been disfigured so badly.

Checkpoint 13

We respond to his voice as narrator but we need to be aware of how others see him. Cormier wants the reader to confront the horrific effects of war. It hurts those we like as well as those we don't.

Checkpoint 14

Francis would want to celebrate Larry's homecoming because like the other young people of Frenchtown he regarded him as a hero already. Before he went to war himself Francis had an idealised view of war heroes as bold and daring men.

Checkpoint 15

The words 'lethal' and 'knife-like' (p. 68) suggest the hardness and danger which lies beneath Larry's handsome exterior.

Checkpoint 16

The word 'gnawing' implies something is worrying him. Francis feels he has no choice because he respects Larry and has to follow his instructions.

Checkpoint 17

Larry might not want to face Nicole and Francis again. He is afraid of being found out and thereby having his image as hero tarnished.

Checkpoint 18

Francis feels he is a fake hero because he wanted to die in the war; he had no intention of saving others, and his actions were guided by his sense of cowardice.

Checkpoint 19

Francis has accomplished his mission because he told Larry that he knew about the rape of Nicole. Larry is about to die which is what Francis wanted, although Francis will not kill him as he intended.

Checkpoint 20

He lost Nicole at the time of the attack when he failed to help her. As readers we feel sympathy for him as in losing Nicole's love he has lost the thing which matters to him most.